ANNIHILATE HIM: HOLIDAY

CHRISTINA ROSS

INTRODUCTION

Annihilate Him: Holiday is a new book set in the *Annihilate Me* universe. It's an extension of the series, with more than 1,500,000 books sold worldwide.

Although this new book can be read on its own, readers will likely enjoy it more if they first read the original *Annihilate Me* series, followed by the *Unleash Me* series, the *Annihilate Him* series, and *Ignite Me*, as it shares the same characters. The experience will be dramatically deepened.

For my friends and my family.

And especially for my readers, who mean the world to me.

Thank you for following all of your favorite characters into a new holiday story.

DISCLAIMER

I visited Sugarloaf mountain several times while I was earning my undergrad degree at the University of Maine before going on to earn my master's degree in English at Columbia University in New York. So, for the purposes of this book, I've turned the Widowmaker Lounge into something far less chaotic than what it is in reality. In this book, it's a calmer place—but one that, nevertheless, is full of hot, single men!

1

_____

IT WAS a frigid December morning and the snow was flying high in midtown when I gave my husband, Alexander Wenn, a kiss on the lips and told him that I loved him.

"I love you, too," Alex said when he returned my kiss. "And by the way, Jennifer—just so you know, you've already got that warrior look in your eyes."

I furrowed my brow at him as our limo pulled alongside the Wenn Enterprises Building on Fifth.

"What 'warrior look'?"

"The determined one that says 'I can move the world with the mere flick of my finger.'"

"Well, I'm nothing short of determined this morning!"

After all, today wasn't going to be just another busy day at the office for me. There was another level to the day that could potentially derail it. I also needed to nail down a commitment from a certain Barbara Blackwell that was going to be trying at best, hellish at worst.

Who knew when it came to that one?

Our head of security, Tank, came out of Wenn and opened the limo's door for us. I stepped out of the car first, and reached up to give him a quick peck on the cheek. "Morning, Tank," I said.

"Good morning, Jennifer. Alex," Tank said with a nod.

"Good to see you, friend," Alex said. "Oh, and if you wouldn't mind turning off the snow, that would be great."

"I'll work on that," Tank said.

"Perfect. And I'll see you at noon?" Alex said.

"Noon for your business lunch at the Four Seasons. I'll meet you in the lobby. Jennifer, Cutter will meet you in the lobby at noon also for your lunch date with Lisa."

"I can't wait to see her," I said. "I haven't seen her in a week. Talking to her on the phone every day isn't the same thing."

"New book and all," he said. "She's been working hard on it."

"Inexcusable. We need our girl time together. If you'd let Cutter know that I'll see him at noon, I'd appreciate it." And then I went in for the kill. "And by the way, *you* look handsome in your suit this morning, Tank. And you know what? Oh, look—it just occurred to me. I can almost see you wearing something just like that when you and Lisa finally pull it together and decide to walk down the aisle. Not that I'm pressuring either of you to make that happen before I die, of course. It's just not in me."

He smiled. I shot him a solid wink, and then Alex and I crossed Fifth's busy sidewalk and moved into the building, the lobby of which was teeming with people moving toward the bank of elevators at the other end of it. My leg muscles were sore from the night before, but I bit down on the pain and moved through it.

"Are you sure you're ready for this?" Alex asked.

"I'm totally ready for this."

"Do you think she'll agree to it?"

"I have zero idea if she'll go for it or not, but as you know, this time I'm well-armed. How can she resist agreeing to our little plan when I show her what I have up my sleeve? She can't. She'll melt when she sees it. When it comes to that one, what I have in store for her will be better than an orgasm. Well... maybe."

"I believe you had a few of those yourself last night."

"In fact, I did."

"By the way, are you OK? You seem a little stiff—it's as if you have a limp."

"After what you did to me last night, I have every right to be walking with a slight limp. Hell, I should be in bed right now with my legs lifted high and wide in stirrups to give everything you pounded against the solid rest it deserves."

He put his hand around my waist, drew me in close to him, and spoke so that only I could hear him. "It's not as if I instigated all of it," he said. "I seem to remember you saying things like 'harder,' 'faster,' 'give it to me, stud,' and 'woo-hoo, look at me, I'm a cowgirl'."

I wanted to laugh out loud, but because so many of our employees were around us, I needed to keep it in check. "I never said that last part."

"Oh, yes, you did."

"Oh, no, I didn't."

"OK, so maybe you didn't."

"But I'm pretty sure that I did call you a stud," I said. "Because, you know, your wife kind of thinks that you're a pretty big one."

With a few other employees, we stepped into one of the elevators. After exchanging greetings with them, Alex and I pressed the buttons for our respective floors and stood at the back of the car holding hands and looking up at the dial as the doors slid shut, and the elevator began its ascent.

Since Madison Wells was to be my partner in crime today, I was getting off on the fortieth floor, where Wenn Entertainment was located and where Madison now worked as an assistant director of marketing in the music division. She'd been in this position since we'd found it for her in June, and Alex and I thought—along with Blackwell herself —that she was thriving in it.

"Off to see Madison," I said to Alex as the elevator dinged. "Wish me luck?"

"Not that you'll need it, my little warrior, but good luck."

Since we tried to keep it as professional as possible at work, we simply squeezed each other's hands goodbye, and when the doors slid open, I was off to find Madison.

MADISON'S OFFICE was down a long hallway already bustling with dozens of people, feeding the space with a strong creative vibe.

Wenn Entertainment oversaw all of Wenn's movie, television, and music ventures. It wasn't often that my job took me here, but whenever it did, I could feel the electricity and excitement in my bones.

After stopping to say hello to a number of people and checking in on their various projects, I reached Madison's door, and knocked.

"Come in," she called.

I stuck my head inside. "Hi," I said.

She spun around in her chair, placed her palms in front of her on her glass desk, and winked at me. "Hi, Jennifer."

She looked not only beautiful, but also more confident than the young woman I'd met just six months ago, when she first came to Wenn as Blackwell's personal assistant. There likely were four other reasons for the change I saw in her now—her relationship with Alex's cousin Brock was becoming increasingly serious, I knew for a fact that she loved her job, she now had the means to dress in ways that finally had earned her Blackwell's approval—and then there was that little something I'd noted on Billboard's site while having my morning coffee.

"Congrats on scoring your first number-one single," I said.

"I can't believe it," she said. "But it was hardly just me. The entire team threw everything they had into getting that song out to radio. Lucky for us, that radio loved it."

"I'm sure that you had a big hand in it. Alex was thrilled when I told him. He specifically said to me, 'Didn't Madison work on that?' I reminded him that you did, so he's fully aware of it."

"Thanks, Jennifer. That means a great deal to me."

"My pleasure." I looked around her office and then lowered my voice. "So—did you get it?"

She stood up from her desk and flashed her eyes at me. "Oh, I so got it. Last night—right after work."

"Let me see it!"

"Close the door. You never know when that one might appear. Yesterday, I was writing a press release and glanced up to find her standing in my doorway, watching me silently with folded arms. She scared the hell out of me."

"Part of her M.O." I said as I closed the door.

"Anyway, I put it over here in my closet. Wait until you see it in person."

And when Madison showed it to me, I knew that the plan she and I had cooked up to sway Blackwell's decision in our favor might just work indeed.

"You remember the plan?" I said to her before we left for Blackwell's floor.

"I remember it."

"Then let's get this done and nail it down."

2

"Hi, Barbara," I said when I reached her office. For the time being, Madison hung back in the hallway and remained strategically out of sight.

"Jennifer," Blackwell said as her gaze swept over me. "Nice suit. Winter white and all that. Fendi is it? Don't answer. I already know that it is. And even though you decided to become some sort of a lab rat and not consult me on it, I have to say that it looks good on you."

"Thank you—I guess..."

"Believe me—take the compliment while you can. And I have to say that you still continue to surprise me. To top it all off, that suit of yours is actually part of this year's fall/winter collection—so be still my heart. Perhaps you're finally learning that last year's fashion really is last year's fashion. God knows you have enough money at your disposal to make *that* a priority—especially since I have to look at you."

"Are we through with the suit?"

"Oh, we're through with it," she said. "Because just by looking at you, I can tell that you're filling my doorway for some sort of unwanted, subversive reason that I have no intention of dealing with right now."

"What does that even mean?"

She removed her narrow black glasses from her face and tossed them onto the desk in front of her. Then, she folded her arms across her chest, leaned back in her chair, and studied me with a peculiar look on her face. Barbara Blackwell was the vice president of human resources at Wenn, and despite how harsh she sometimes came off, at this point, I knew that most of it was just a façade. She was a mother figure to me.

"Why are you here?" she asked. "And when you first said hello to me, why was that horrid, yet oh-so-familiar note back in your voice?"

"What horrid note?"

"The one you use whenever you want something from me. Do you have any idea that when you use it that you sound like Snow White, for God's sake? 'Hi, Barbara'," she said in a sweet, lilting voice that mimicked mine. "God! Whenever I hear you sound like that, I half expect blue birds to fly out of your ass and flutter around whatever's in that head of yours. So, what is it? Clearly, you're up to something."

As long as I'd known Blackwell, I'd yet to figure out how to outwit her. It was infuriating to me. Was there nothing this woman didn't see coming?

"Well," I said.

"Just spit it out."

"Fine. Christmas is a week away. Alex and I were talking the other night, and we decided that we'd ask—"

"Oh, no," she said. "Not that again. Not ever. Not. Even. Going. To. Happen."

"Just hear me out?"

"And yet suddenly I've gone deaf."

"The hell you have. We are inviting you, Daniella, and Alexa to join Alex and me, along with Brock, Madison, and Cutter, in Maine for Christmas this year. No arguments. Last year was an unmitigated success."

"Really, Jennifer? An unmitigated success? Do you even remember how Alexa and Daniella tore into each other during those few days?"

"They weren't that bad."

"The lies!"

"Fine—they had their moments. Those two will always have their moments. But do I need to remind you that they certainly found a way to come together when we were stranded on that island this summer? Daniella actually cared for her sister at one point. They might not often show it, but as different as they are, they do love each other, and they do have a bond. If they could make it through what happened to us on that island, then they certainly can manage spending the holidays together in Maine with us again."

"They had no choice but to make it on that island. Their lives were at stake, for God's sake. And now you're telling me that Cutter will be there? The Cutter who remains single to this day? What in the fresh hell do you think Daniella is going to do with that?"

"Whenever she's tried to hit on Cutter—like when she got on bended knee and asked him to marry her—he's always handled her with poise and kindness."

"Well, I will admit to that. You know I love that boy. After what he did for all of us on that island, he's a gift. And if Daniella would grow the hell up and get her act together, I would love to have him as a son-in-law. But that's not going to happen, because I think that an unmedicated Daniella is forever going to be unhinged. As much as I love my daughter, I know that Cutter deserves better. And by the way, why didn't you mention Lisa and Tank? Have you become so cold and self-involved that you decided to cut them out of the festivities?"

"Of course they were invited—do you really think that I wouldn't invite them?"

"Crystals of ice embrace your heart in ways that are deeply concerning to me," she said.

I rolled my eyes and pressed on. "Tank is taking Lisa home to Prairie Home, Nebraska to finally meet his parents this Christmas."

"To where?"

"To Prairie Home—"

"I heard you. I just can't believe that a mountain of a man like Tank comes from someplace called Prairie Home, Nebraska. But since a wedding has to come at some point, I suppose it's about time that she meets them, and that they become acquainted with her zombies."

"There's that," I said. "Anyway, since we are a family—and because you are my surrogate womb—"

"Would you please stop using that term? It's grotesque."

"—Alex and I, along with Cutter, Brock, and Madison, want you, Daniella, and Alexa to pack your bags and join us for another holiday. We leave in five days. We'll arrive on the twenty-second. We'll settle in. We'll celebrate. We'll eat. We'll ski. And we'll even exchange gifts. And then, the day after Christmas, we'll be on a flight home to New York so the girls can still hang out with their friends on New Year's Eve. How bad can that be? It's only for four days."

Blackwell simply looked at me with a bemused smile.

"Jennifer," she said. "Darling," she said. "I do love you. But if you think for one moment that my daughters or I am going back to that horrible hellhole of a cottage Alex and you call your 'second home' on that raw and ugly coast of Maine for yet another Christmas gathering, well, you can forget about that right now. It's not going to happen."

"We're not going to our house on the Point," I said to her. "And by the way, that house is as lovely as its views. And I believe that you spent plenty of time there with Alex's mother when she was alive. It's no hellhole. You're just acting up, as you usually do. That said—and in case you didn't hear me the first time, allow me to repeat—we aren't going there. Alex has already secured a cabin for us at Sugarloaf."

"A cabin?" she said, lifting her dark bob away from her face with the pinky of her right hand. "So, now I'm to become some sort of a woodswoman? Should I bring a rifle with me? Should I learn to shoot? Bare knives? Swords? Sling arrows? Seriously, Jennifer? A cabin? Get real."

"That's just what they call them there," I said. "What Alex chose for us is large and elegant. And, by the way, he did all of this out of love for his family, which includes you, Daniella, and Alexa."

"Why would he ever choose a place called 'Sugarloaf'?" she said. "Already it sounds fattening. I'm imagining a heaping dose of sugar folded into loaves of bread. Are you trying to fatten me up? Just hearing this revelation of yours makes me want to crack down on a few cubes of ice." And when she said that, her gaze roamed over my body. "As should you, my dear. Because, you know, if a baby is to come for you and Alex, which I believe it will sooner rather than later at the rate you two are going at it, you need to start to control your weight right now. And just by looking at you, I'd say that you're failing spectacularly."

"Like hell I am."

"Oh, you've gained a few ounces. Believe me on that."

"Moving on. Sugarloaf is one of the best ski resorts in the United States."

"A ski resort," she said. "So, now you're expecting me to ski?"

"I actually think you'll rather enjoy it."

"Then you clearly know nothing about me."

"Oh, but I do know you. And do you want to know how well I know you? Why don't I just show you? Madison?" I called out.

"You've brought Madison into this?" Blackwell said.

"In fact I have, because, along with the rest of us, she wants you and the girls to join us."

Madison entered the room with a garment bag that was branded with the 'Chanel' logo.

"Hello, Barbara," she said.

"'Hello,' my ass. And what is that you're carrying?"

"Enticement," Madison said.

"I don't even know what that means..."

"Jennifer and I thought that if you were to take to the slopes—even the bunny slopes, which are super easy and fun—that you might want to rock them in this."

"The bunny slopes," Blackwell said. "What is this? The seventies? That sounds like *Playboy* to me. Utter porn! But whatever. I'm already starting to become weirdly transfixed by the Chanel logo. So, reveal to me what's inside—if it even is from Chanel..."

"It is," Madison said, pulling down the zipper and removing the bright red, quilted ski suit we'd purchased for Blackwell at Chanel. "And not only is it your size, but no one is going to be wearing anything like this in Maine."

The moment Blackwell saw it, she stood.

"Turn it for me," she said.

Madison turned it this way and that.

"It's sublime," she said. "Perfection." She shot me a look. "I don't follow ski suits, so I need to know—is this part of this year's collection?"

"It is," I said. "It's bright red, it's leather, and it's to die for."

"And there also are these," Madison said as she reached deep into the bag. "Sun goggles—also by Chanel. Just look at the solar finish on them. Hypnotizing! And then there are the gloves," she said, retrieving them from the bottom of the bag. "Black. To create a shot of interest and, you know, to match your boots. When you're in this, you will be the star of the slopes."

"The star," Blackwell said. "How enticing. Let me touch it!"

When she did, she looked at each of us.

"Fine. Let me see what I can do with the girls," she said. "At this point, I must say that I appreciate your slovenly holiday appeal. But none of this is a done deal yet. Naturally, the Chanel is divoon. And frankly, when it came to targeting your audience—which naturally was me—you did an outstanding job. But I'll nevertheless need to get back to you on all of this, because, despite how desperately each of you have groveled, I remain unconvinced about whether we'll go until my daughters weigh in."

3

LISA and I met for lunch in the Pool Room at the Four Seasons. Traffic was ridiculous due to the light bit of snow we'd received, so I was a full ten minutes late. I'd sent Lisa a text on the drive over, so at least she was expecting me to be late.

"Ms. Ward is sitting right over there, Mrs. Wenn," the maître d' said as he led me into the lavish space after checking my coat.

"Thank you, Stephen."

"Always my pleasure. You two do tend to lift the room. In fact, I'd say that right now that you alone are attracting your share of attention."

Since I could see heads turning toward me as I followed him deeper into the restaurant, I knew what he meant, not that I commented on it. I couldn't care less about how well known I was in this city. And so we just carried on, stepping past the square pool at our left, which was illumined from within and giving off a warm glow of light. Lisa was sitting at a table along the wall of windows at the opposite end of the room. Her face brightened when she saw me.

"Finally," she said, standing up to give me a hug.

"It's been a full week," I said. "And by the way, enough of this. We should be seeing each other twice a week. Certainly we can manage that."

"The undead shall see to it," she said.

When we parted and sat down, Stephen asked us if we'd like something to drink.

"Martini," I said. "Three olives. Same for that one."

"Belvedere?"

"Perfect," Lisa said. "Just make sure it's as smooth as silk and as cold as January."

"You remember that?" I said to her.

"Are you joking? That's one of the most elegant lines I've ever heard. I remember the day that Ann said that to you. It was when you first met Alex. And look at how that turned out."

"I'd say pretty damned well. How are you, lovecat? You look fresh!"

"If I do, it's nothing short of a goddamned zombie miracle. The new book is killing me, but we'll talk about that later—because I might have something to share with you that's funny and scandalous, but that could get me into a bit of trouble. It involves my new book—and it involves Blackwell."

"You've put Blackwell into your book?"

"Not getting into specifics quite yet."

"What? How can this even be? You're going to tease me with that and leave me hanging?"

"It's called a hook," Lisa said. "It's what we writers do. But it'll be worth it. Hell, it might even be dessert!"

"Now I totally need to know."

"Later. First thing's first—did Blackwell cave in? Are she

and the girls going to go to Maine with you for the holidays?"

"I think the Chanel ski-suit stunt worked, but she still needs to get buy-in from Alexa and Daniella, who are nothing if not difficult. So I'll know by the end of the day or tomorrow morning."

"Good luck with those two if they do decide to go."

"It can't be as bad as last year," I said.

"Really? From what you told me, Cutter is going to be there. Daniella's hormones are going to circle around him like a blizzard of buzzards. Good for you for trying to enjoy some Christmas cheer and all that, but I think that you're in for it."

"Look, it is what it is—they're family to me at this point. They need to be there. The only thing that will be missing are Tank and you. I wish you were coming, but I understand why you aren't. Do you realize that this will be the first Christmas we haven't spent together?"

"I'm still trying to process it."

"It's just not going to be the same."

"It's not, but it's time for me to meet the family!" she said in a completely false yet light-hearted voice. "And we'll see if those Midwesterners take a liking to me or not."

"They'll love you."

"I write about zombies, Jennifer. They'll probably think that they need to serve me a raw steak or something."

"I have a feeling that Tank's family is far more sensitive and advanced than that."

"I'm just joking. I actually can't wait to meet them—I mean, they produced Tank. How bad can they be? That said, we have to spend the entire week at their house! And Tank said that it isn't a large house. And all of us know what that means. If he even tries to have sex with me, *his parents will hear my every moan and groan!*"

"Oh, dear. Well, my best advice is to exhaust him before you leave."

"Seriously? Tank has conditioned himself to the point that he's essentially a machine. We might have to do what you and Alex pulled last Christmas. You know—escape to a no-tell motel, just to have some sort of privacy together. Hopefully, there's a motel nearby. In fact, I need to Google that shit STAT. If there is one close to us, we'll just say, 'Hey, look at us, we're just going to do some shopping! See you soon! And by the way, don't mind me if I return looking as if your son has just banged the hell out of me, because he will have. Pay no attention!'"

"You're killing me."

When a waiter returned with our martinis and asked us if we would like to order, I declined. "If you don't mind, we'd first like to enjoy our drinks and catch up, and then we'll order."

"Absolutely, Mrs. Wenn. Just catch my eye when you're ready, and I'll be right over."

"Thank you."

When he walked away, Lisa said, "People fucking revere you."

"Oh, they do not."

"Like hell they don't."

"You've had two number-one bestsellers in a row. As if people don't revere you as well."

"My peeps just want to eat my brains. And other body parts. That's the crowd I'm selling to. You, on the other hand, have become New York royalty. And by the way," she said, leaning into me. "How are things going with the pregnancy thing? Is New York any closer to having its newest prince or princess?"

My shoulders slumped. "Alex and I are trying like a couple of type-A overachievers to get pregnant, but nothing has happened yet. In fact, I took a test this morning, because I knew that we'd be having our usual martinis and there was no way in hell I wasn't going to have one if the results were negative, which they were. I'm starting to become desperate. I don't understand why I'm not pregnant yet. My doctor continues to tell me that I'm fine. That it will happen. But it's been seven months, Lisa, and I'm starting to wonder if there's a problem."

"Seven months is fine," she said. "I've already done my research on the sly. There might be an issue when it takes you longer than a year to conceive. At that point, you might want to seek out some sort of assistance. But I'm not concerned. You'll get that bun in your oven soon enough, and you'll bake it to perfection. The time will choose itself, Jennifer. But I hear you. And I'm just as frustrated for you as you are. I know that, since your miscarriage, you and Alex have become more committed than ever to having a child. So, let's lift our glasses and give cheer to the day when that happens," she said. "Because it's going to come soon."

We touched glasses and sipped our martinis.

"Damn that's good," Lisa said.

"It's nothing like the rotgut we used to drink when we first arrived in the city, that's for sure."

"I don't even want to remember those days."

"Actually, I do. It makes me appreciate everything I have now—and I'm not talking about material things. I could give a damn about those. I'm talking about my husband, you and Tank, Blackwell, and my other new friends. They're the ones who mean the most to me."

"Well, when you put it like that, I'm just as grateful. Next to you, Tank is one of the best things that has ever happened to me. Thank you for introducing me to him—even if I did look like a slut when we first met. But whatever—wearing no bra in a white tank top did the trick!"

"To say the least. So, I have to ask, it's been nearly a year since you two became engaged. When are you going to marry?"

"Actually—and this is on the low down, so keep your lips sealed—discussions are underway."

"And you've told me nothing about this?"

"He only brought it up to me a few days ago. I wanted to tell you in person."

"Tank brought it up?"

"In fact, he did!"

"Shit's about to get real."

"I know! He said that we should set a date because he wants to start calling me his 'wife.' And how romantic is that?"

"I love him."

"Everyone loves Tank—he's the best. How lucky am I?"

"You're both lucky. So, when's the date?"

"I've always wanted to be a June bride, and I think that's going to happen. If, you know, I pass the parent test. Because if I don't? What are we to do then?"

"Get married," I said. "To hell with them if they don't like you, not that I see that happening. In fact, I think they're going to fall in love with you. Despite your zombies."

"Here's the catch," she said. "From what Tank has told me, I'm pretty sure that they're totally religious, so we're going to have to wait and see about that. Who knows how they'll react to me? And what I do for work? I'm taking their only child for God's sake. And I write best-selling novels about the undead. What will the peeps in Prairie Home, Nebraska think of that?"

"Yeah, there's that," I said. "So! I think we need another drink!"

"I agree."

And so we drank.

LATER, after we'd ordered, I turned the conversation back to Lisa's new book. "All right," I said. "Spill it about the new book. What does Blackwell have to do with it?"

"I totally need you to have my back when it comes to this one," she said.

"What does that mean?"

"Because my veiled reference to her in the new book isn't really that, well, veiled at all..."

"Sweet Jesus!"

"So, here's what I've done. I've got this minor character named Bertha. She just has a small part, but she kind of steals the show."

"Already I can't stand it."

"Then buckle up, lady. Because before Bertha was turned, she was a total fashionista. A big corporate power-house who loved her some Chanel."

"Please, God, no."

"Oh, please, God, yes! Anyway, Bertha gets bitten by some poor infected beast and becomes a zombie. Then, because some part of her remembers that she loves couture, she starts raiding all of the Chanel stores in Manhattan."

"On, no, she doesn't!"

"Oh, yes, she does! She goes to the Chanel on East 57th Street, and then to the one on Madison Avenue, and finally she marches her bony, rotting ass to the one on Spring Street. And in between, there's Bergdorf and Saks! It's pure satire, but I think that it's just funny and subversive enough for my readership to enjoy. Here is a zombie who has somehow remembered what she loved most when she was alive—fashion. And also the need to look her best, regardless of the fact that she's been reduced to a decaying corpse. Blackwell has always wanted to be as thin as a needle, so I've given Bertha the same traits. She's a knot of bones with not a lick of meat on them. As she goes from store to store, she tries on this Chanel suit, this Chanel jacket, that Chanel dress, those Chanel shoes. She actually goes from a size zero to a minus two. To top it off, she decides which tailors live or die—if only so that her clothes can be fitted properly to her."

"Why do I feel like cackling?" I said.

"Because we both know that if this was indeed Blackwell, it is the zombie she'd turn out to be."

"Iris is going to have your ass."

"Are you kidding me? You know how Iris and Blackwell are together. Iris isn't just an excellent editor, but she also has one serious sense of humor. I think she's going to have a gas when she reads that passage. It's only a few pages, but it does make a social statement about our must-have-everything culture. I'm just grateful to Blackwell for the inspiration."

"Well," I said. "As horrified and as delighted as I am, cheers to you, my friend. Because that shit is funny."

"Just don't say a word of it to anyone."

"Like I would—I'm a vault. So, when do you and Tank leave?"

"Two days," she said.

"So you'll be back before New Year's?"

"We will."

"Then the four of us will need to spend New Year's Eve together," I said. "I'll nail down a restaurant for us. If you have any ideas, shoot them my way. As for the men in our lives, they could give a rat's ass about where we go. But I want to play dress up with you, so it needs to be somewhere super fancy."

"I'm totally on board with that. And since you are absolutely revered in this town, you can make that happen."

"I'm not even going to respond to that, because you're just baiting me. Here's what I say—the day before the big night, we'll go shopping for new dresses."

"Maybe Bertha won't mind helping us out with that," Lisa said.

"You're terrible—and I love you for it," I said. "And look, try to have a good time with Tank and his parents. They'll fall in love with you—I know they will. And do your best to find a nearby no-tell motel so that you and Tank can have some alone time. And then come back to me and Alex so we can end this ruinous year on one mother of a positive note."

When I said that, my cell phone dinged in my purse.

"Who's that?" Lisa asked. "Oh, I know—likely a love note from Alex."

"He's having a business lunch, so it can't be him. Let me check." I removed the phone and looked at the screen. "It's a text from Blackwell," I said.

"Here comes your answer, so gird your loins, lovey."

When I read the text, I felt a sense of relief as well as a sense of foreboding. "They're in," I said to Lisa. "Though apparently there are provisions."

"Here's my guess—they want to know where they're staying, and if each girl gets their own bedroom and bathroom."

"Why do you say that?"

"Because I know those girls."

"Well, if that's the issue, the good news is that they will get both this year. Alex secured a huge house for us that overlooks Big Bear Lake. You remember going to the Loaf when we were in college—that spot is beautiful. Bars and restaurants are within walking distance, and the mountain itself is just minutes away by car. We're smack in the middle of everything."

Lisa lifted her martini to her lips. "Then it looks to me like this is happening," she said. "And hopefully it won't age you. As much as I wish that Tank and I could be with you, there are now two concrete reasons why I'm very happy that we won't be—Alexa and Daniella. Oh, and lest I forget, there's also Cutter, whom Daniella threw herself at in ways that none of us will ever forget. So, honey, girlfriend, chica —you know. When Daniella starts to go gaga over him? Good luck with all that!"

4

WHEN I RETURNED to Wenn later that afternoon after a fabulous lunch with Lisa and an emotional farewell as we went our separate ways for the holidays, I went straight to Blackwell's office to lock down our own holiday plans.

"I'm so glad that you've agreed to come!" I said when I stepped into her office.

"Well, that's something I haven't heard in years," she said as she patted her bob. "And God knows Charles was always just as surprised as I was when it actually happened. He was a terrible lover."

"You're the one who's terrible."

"Oh, look—words I've never heard before." She pointed a finger at me. "By the way, I've agreed to nothing yet. We need to cover a few things first. I have questions."

I sat down in the chair opposite her. "Ask away."

"Daniella and Alexa want separate bedrooms and bathrooms. Is that going to happen this time?"

Man, did Lisa ever nail that or what?

"In fact, they will. That should make them happy. As I said, at the Loaf—"

"At the what?"

"Most people call Sugarloaf 'the Loaf.'"

"Well, already that sounds better to me, because right there—we've already cut out half the calories."

"Anyway," I said with a sigh, "back to the cabin, which isn't even a cabin. It's a freaking mansion. Alex rented us a monstrosity that's just over nine-thousand square feet. Is that large enough for everyone? It certainly should be, because I've seen photos of it and it's huge. It's also in the middle of everything. The slopes are close. The bars, shops, and restaurants are literally within walking distance. We'll be overlooking Big Bear Lake, which is so expansive, it looks as if you're overlooking the ocean—but without the salty smell you seem to dislike."

"Because it can be rancid."

"Only when it's at low tide."

"Haven't you noticed? I'm not a low-tide kind of girl."

And...I'm just moving on!

"Alex has arranged to have everything decorated for the holidays before we arrive. We're really trying to please everyone here, Barbara. What else can we offer?"

"Nothing," she said in a softer tone. "And I have to say that the girls and I appreciate the effort, the thought, the invitation, and the work that has gone into making all this just right. Just so you know, I was on board the moment you mentioned it to me, because I do want to spend the holidays with you. After all, Alex and you are my family. But as you know all too well, my girls aren't such an easy sell. That said, now that I know that their conditions have been met, we would love to spend the holidays with Alex and you, as well as with Cutter, Brock, and Madison. I just wish that Lisa and Tank were coming. Even though I understand that it's time for her to meet his parents, it still won't seem right without them."

"Tell me about it," I said. "This will be the first time since I've known Lisa that we haven't spent the holidays together. Oh, and by the way, I just had lunch with her—I have news."

"What news? How could it be that I haven't heard of this news before you?"

"Because I'm her best friend?"

"Whatever. Spill it."

"She and Tank are getting close to setting a date!"

"Well, it's about time," Blackwell said. "Let's just call it what it is—a goddamned Christmas miracle. Do you know when?"

"She is cagey about setting the exact date, but she did say that she's always wanted to be a June bride—which I've known since we were kids. So, I think a wedding will happen in June."

"In June?" Blackwell said. "But that's only six months away. Does that girl have any idea of the sheer amount of time it takes to pull together a proper wedding? One should spend a year organizing such an event."

I just shrugged at her. "Alex and I got married in his office on the sly," I said. "What in the hell do I know about having a big wedding?"

"Nothing. What Alex and you did still ruins me to this day. To deny me of seeing you in a proper dress. Hell, each of you having a proper ceremony. And to deny your friends of enjoying in the same. It was cruel."

"And yet here we are—stronger than ever," I said.

"And that you are. But as for Lisa and Tank, I might need to get involved if this is going to take place in June."

"I think that she'd enjoy that."

"But would her mother?"

"Probably not so much..."

"Fine then. But I have to ask—what in the hell does her mother, who hails from the barns of Maine, know about putting on a big New York wedding? Zip! Just let Lisa know that I'm available should she need me. You know, such as when it comes to the mere incidental of finding the right dress. The right caterer. The right florist. The right church. The right space for the reception. The list goes on and on. Does her mother know Manhattan's best of the best in the ways that I do? I think we both know the answer to that question. While I'm sure that Lisa comes from a fine family, I'd bet my life on the fact that her mother would struggle to find the right people to coordinate her wedding here in New York."

"Assuming that they get married in New York," I said.

"Do you think that they wouldn't?"

"I'm not sure. Like I said, I know nothing at this point. But let's not worry about that now. Let's deal with the upcoming holiday. Tank and Lisa leave in two days. We leave in five. I don't know about you, but I've been so busy, I haven't even started my Christmas shopping yet. Have you?"

"To a point I have, but that point hardly ends with an exclamation point. There is still plenty of ground to be covered, especially since I now know that I need to find gifts for Cutter, Brock, and Madison. And believe me when I tell you this, my dear. After this year? After the way he assisted us on that island? I am going to smother Cutter in particular with gifts."

"The same goes for me and Alex—what Cutter doesn't know is that Alex and I are going to give him a huge year-end bonus. Same goes for Tank. Still, I have to say that I wish that Cutter and Susan hadn't broken up. I understand why they did—she received a killer job offer in Chicago, and she would have been a fool to pass that up. But because of that, Cutter isn't going to have anyone special to spend the holidays with. Yes, on paper, he's officially going to be there to be our security detail. But we both know that's not really the case. He's going to be there because he's a member of our extended family. We need to make a real effort to make this Christmas special for him."

"I agree," she said. "Let me call Alexa and Daniella now to get their full buy-in. And if they *are* in, how about if you and I go shopping for all involved?"

"Oh, I'd love that," I said.

"Why wouldn't you? For the love of Chanel, you'd have me on your arm to guide you on what to buy and what to pass on. Let me call them."

When she explained to the girls that they'd have not only their own bedrooms, but also separate bathrooms, they got immediately on board.

"So, that's done," Blackwell said when she put down her cell. "I guess we'll be spending the holidays together after all. And that makes me very happy. But don't you dare expect me to cook for you again."

"I don't."

"You don't?"

"No, I don't."

"Well, you certainly said *that* quickly—perhaps even too quickly. Do you even remember the magic I created last year, Jennifer? That meal I cooked for us was divoon. And do you want to know why? It's because that fat Contessa got me through all of it."

"And it was delicious," I said. "I just don't want you to be bothered with having to prepare Christmas dinner again. Madison and I will tend to it. And if Daniella or Alexa want to join in, the more the merrier."

"Rest assured, that won't happen when it comes to those two. Daniella won't do it because Daniella is Daniella. Alexa won't do it because she's a vegetarian and will be repelled to see a dead turkey ready to be stuffed. So, if you and Madison will take my place this year for that chore, I'd be grateful for it—but I'm here to tell you that it's going to be hellish! When I was making the stuffing alone, I was certain at one point that it started to look like a placenta to me. It was disgusting."

"But it tasted so good," I said.

"Again," she said. "That fat Contessa came through for me." She leaned forward. "And maybe this year she'll come through for you."

5

OVER THE NEXT THREE DAYS, Blackwell and I shopped—and we shopped hard. We went to Saks, to Bergdorf, to Tiffany, to Prada, to Chanel, to Dior, to Barneys and to Bloomingdale's, and then to Louis Vuitton, Henri Bendel, and beyond. When we'd finally ticked off everything on our list and all of our packages had been professionally wrapped, we had Cutter drop me off at Alex and my apartment on Fifth.

After pulling the limousine alongside the apartment building, Cutter stepped out and began to tell the doormen which packages were to be delivered to me. I reached over and gave Blackwell a kiss on each cheek.

"There you go again," she said. "Spreading germs."

"Germs aside, I suggest that you get your rest. Because I can tell you right now, Barbara, that you're going to need it. You think that island was tough? Wait until you strap on a set of skis and take to the slopes."

"Why in hell have I agreed to any of this?"

"Because Madison and I got you with the Chanel ski suit, goggles, and gloves that you'll soon wear."

"Well, there's that," she said.

"And because you wouldn't have it any other way."

"I suppose there's that, too."

"Be ready by nine," I said. "We're taking one of Wenn's Lears at noon, and will arrive in Bangor an hour later. Then, it's about a two-hour drive to the Loaf. Once we're there, we'll all get settled in, and then we'll have dinner before calling it a night and hitting the slopes the next day."

"Already it sounds exhausting," she said. "I might just decide to drink in the dark. Alone. Cold, unwanted, and bitter."

"The hell you will. Do you have any idea what that suit cost me, let alone the gloves and the goggles?"

"As if you couldn't afford it."

"Still!"

"And by the way, I already looked it up to see what I was worth to you. So, you know, well done, darling. Well done."

"You did not look up how much it costs..."

"Of course I did. If I'm going to get my ass on those bunny slopes, I needed to see what else Chanel had up their sleeves in case I wanted to bring something else along. But I have to say that you and Madison chose exactly right. The suit is perfection. And by the way, Jennifer, don't think that I won't make a marathon of those bunny slopes just because I'm older than you. I plan to conquer them!"

"What a surprise. But I'm happy that you're up for the challenge—"

"Challenge?" she interrupted. "I don't consider any of this a challenge. Those slopes will bend over backwards for me."

"Will they?" I asked.

"What does that mean?"

"I'm just wondering if you've ever skied before."

"No, but I've certainly seen people ski on TV. During the

Olympics. You know, that sort of thing. *J'adore* the figure skating! Just watching those skaters alone makes me long to do the triple salchow, axel, and lutz. To me, those moves look difficult and dangerous. But skiing? It can't be that hard. Everyone makes it look so easy."

Oh, bloody hell, she is so going to have my ass when she finds out that there's nothing easy about one's first time skiing...

"Well, we'll see," I said brightly. "And by the way, that's the spirit, old girl!"

"Old girl my ass."

"Anyway, I need to see my husband, who has barely seen me since we started this three-day shopping spree of ours. We also need to pack for our time away, and I imagine that you and the girls need to do the same."

"The girls?" she said. "Please. I not only have to pack for me, but if they're in one of their moods, I'll likely need to pack for them as well. So, you are correct—scram. I need to get things done if we're to leave at nine."

When I left her and moved onto the sidewalk, I gave Cutter a quick peck on the cheek.

"I'm so glad that you're coming," I said. "And while I know that officially you're coming for work, you must know that it means much more than that to all of us, Cutter. We want you with us. We want you to spend the holidays with us. Consider this a working vacation with your extended family. Because, as far as I'm concerned, you are my family."

He was so tall, he had to smile down at me. "I appreciate that—and I feel the same, Jennifer. If I didn't have you and Alex—and everyone else— I would have been spending Christmas visiting a few buddies of mine, and all of them are married with children. So, I'm grateful for the invitation and am looking forward to whatever comes of it."

"You're talking about Daniella right now, aren't you?"

He was such a gentleman, he didn't answer.

"Look, I'll keep her in line," I said. "Well, knowing Daniella, at least I'll try my best. But that might not be worth a damn when it comes to her..."

"I'm not worried about Daniella, Jennifer. I actually like her. She just needs the right man to settle her down—and at some point, he'll come along. So, until tomorrow?" he said.

"As in nine o'clock tomorrow. We'll all meet here, and then we'll be on our way." I stopped cold when I said that and just looked at him. "You do ski, don't you?"

"Ski?" he said. "Wait until you see how well I can ski. When I hit the slopes? I'll be giving all of you a run for your money."

Cutter had never been that direct with me—but when he went there, I loved it at once. Because what it said to me was that after all we'd been through together, we were finally coming to a tipping point where he didn't just see me as his employer, but also as his friend.

So, I decided to engage him.

"Is that a challenge?" I asked. "Because I've skied my entire life."

"Then consider it a challenge."

"Well then, bring it on, big boy. Because I'm going to beat your ass on those slopes."

"Sorry," he said. "But that's just not going to happen."

"Oh, my God! It is so game on between us!"

"Do you *really* want to go there?" he asked. "Because I'm that good."

"I'm already there—because I'm fairly certain that I'm better."

"Then you're going to lose. Sorry, Jennifer. But you're going down."

"Like hell I am. But I can tell you this—shit is about to *go* down, and hallelujah for that! This is exactly the kind of competition I needed to go into this week. So, get your game face on, Cutter, because Jen-Jen the ski Jen is about to come after you. Now, get Blackwell home, pack if you haven't already done so, and please get some sleep. Because— believe me when I say this, my friend—I have a feeling that you're going to need it. When you and I go head to head on those slopes? Here's the truth, Cookie Cutter—"

"Cookie Cutter?" he said with a laugh.

"That's right—Cookie Cutter. You've challenged me, and right now? Right now, I'm trying to talk 'street.'"

"OK, 'street.' So, talk."

"All right—so, back into character. I'm going to whip your ass on those slopes!"

"Not happening."

"Please! I started skiing when I was seven. I skied straight through high school and college. You are so about to get schooled, my Navy SEAL—and in two days, you and I are going to go head-to-head in one mother of a fight to the end!"

"Bring it on," he said.

"Oh, it has so just been brought on. I'm coming after you. I'm the Muhammad Ali of the slopes. I will crush you."

"We'll see about that," he said. "Because it's not really about the talk, is it, Jennifer? It's about the results. And I've been skiing as long as you have. I'm also built like a brick shithouse. So, we'll see how it plays out between us. But as for now? I need to get Blackwell home before she has my ass. So, why don't *you* rest up? Because I think that you're the one who's going to need it."

∾

WHEN I ENTERED OUR APARTMENT, I saw that all of the packages had already been delivered and were stacked neatly in the foyer so they could easily be removed when we left in the morning.

"Alex?" I called out while I took off my overcoat.

"In the living room," he said.

"I've missed you!"

"The question is whether you've missed me as much as I've missed you."

"Let's call it a tie."

"Done," I heard him say.

I hung up my coat in the closet and then walked into the living room and joined him on the sofa. He was still in his suit, though his tie had been loosened and in his hand was a martini.

"Would you like a sip?" he asked.

"Indeed, I would."

He held out the glass just in front of my lips. I took a sip, and was quickly convinced that I needed one of my own.

"Let me get one for myself," I said.

"No need—I've already got you covered. Just sit where you are, beautiful. I'll be back in a minute."

As he got up from the sofa and moved into the kitchen area, I thought, *Could I love that man any more? No. It's an impossibility.*

When he returned, he had a freshly made martini ready for me.

"That was quick."

"It's been waiting in the freezer for you."

"You're the best," I said, touching my glass to his before we each took a sip. "My God, what a day. Shopping with Blackwell is like running a marathon."

"So I saw when the doormen delivered the packages. I just hope that all of it fits on the plane."

"It'll fit."

"I'm not so convinced. We might need to take one of the larger planes."

"We'll see," I said. "How did your day go?"

"Just some final touches here and there to close out the year, but now I'm free. Tomorrow, we are out of here, and when we return, this past year will be in the rearview mirror —and we can look forward to what will hopefully be a better year."

"Nothing can be worse than this year."

"Agreed. So, how did the shopping go with Blackwell?"

"I might have cut into Wenn's fourth-quarter earnings..."

He laughed at that, and drew me closer to him. "Whatever it takes for a good holiday," he said. "I could give a damn about what any of it costs. All of us went through hell this year. The SlimPhone continues to be a success, Stephen Rowe is out of our lives, and Wenn is back on top. I say that we all deserve whatever you and Blackwell came up with." He shot me a look. "And what *I* might have come up with..."

"You've gone shopping?"

"A few days ago, when you were having lunch with Lisa, you thought that I was having a business lunch. That was a white lie—but only because I couldn't tip you off. Believe me—you'll forgive me when my own gifts have been revealed. I just wanted to do things on my own without anyone knowing about it."

"But now I *do* know about it."

"Only because I don't like holding on to a fib, even if it means no one any harm. So, now you know. And now it's officially going to eat away at you until Christmas morning, when I show you what I've been up to."

"Now I'm itching to know. But you already knew that I would be when you sprang this on me. You're playing with me."

"How about if I really play with you?" he asked.

I took a long pull from my martini as I noted the look of desire in his eyes, and from that look alone, I knew exactly what was coming my way. And I was happy for it. I didn't know the exact layout of the house he'd rented and if the master bedroom was far and away from the other bedrooms, so I wanted to be as intimate with Alex as I could before we left.

"Mr. Wenn," I said, with a hand to my breasts. "I'm not at all sure what you mean when you say that you want to 'play' with me. I'm just a modest girl in your employ."

"If you're so modest, then why did you urge me to slap you on the ass last night?"

"Surely, that must have been somebody else. It couldn't have been me. I'm just a poor, simple girl from Maine who was raised Catholic."

"Sorry—but I'd never forget that ass of yours. It was you."

"I swear on my rosary beads that it wasn't. But to be honest, Mr. Wenn, for reasons that I can't explain, I have to say that a good-looking man in a business suit does certain things to me that I don't fully understand. I look to God for answers, but none come. And yet still, for some reason, seeing you looking like that tends to make me feel a little, you know, confused because I suddenly become so warm. And moist where I should never, ever be moist. And while I know that it's a sacrilege to admit it, I might even have unwanted thoughts of becoming a little bit wild with you."

"Then finish your drink," he said. "Let's get that fine Catholic ass of yours into the bedroom, and get wild."

And we did.

After downing the rest of our drinks and placing our empty glasses on the coffee table, Alex stood, and in one fell swoop, swept me into his arms, and carried me into our bedroom.

"Are you taking me to where good girls get their presents?" I asked.

"Let's just say that God just answered your call, because I've been waiting for this all day."

When he put me down next to the bed, he removed his suit jacket and then his shirt. With the city light shining against him, I couldn't quite make out the expression on his face, but I could hear plenty in the low growl of his voice when he told me what he planned to do to me. And because of that alone, I could feel the heat building between us as if someone had just set fire to the room.

"The joking is over," I said to him as I undressed. "Do what you want to me."

"Whatever I want?"

I threw my bra against his face—and then my panties. "Whatever you want."

"You might regret that, you know?"

"And I think that you might be underestimating me."

"Christ, I love you," he said.

"Then show me in ways that I'll show you."

When we were naked, he took me into his arms, leaned me down onto the bed, and our mouths became one. I felt his hardness throbbing against my thighs in ways that thrilled me. When I kissed him, I took the back of his head, grabbed a fistful of his hair, and pressed his mouth even closer to mine, to the point that our tongues became one and intertwined.

And then Alex's mouth was gone from mine as he

smoothed his way down my body to my sex, where his tongue plunged deep within it. I let out a primal moan as he started to lick my folds to prepare me for his length and girth, which, even to this day, was still something of a challenge for me to handle.

I writhed beneath his touch and arched my back when he nearly brought me to orgasm, but before that could happen, he was back on top of me again. His mouth was on one of my nipples, and when he bit down on it, I reached out to clutch the bedspread, letting him claim me for his own.

As long as we'd been together—and as many times as we'd made love—he always found ways to make our lovemaking seem fresh, new, and exciting to me. Tonight, it was how he pressed his tongue against the entrance to my buttocks, which was new yet somehow tantalizing to me. But he didn't go there—thank God—because I wasn't quite ready for that. Given his size, I wasn't sure that I'd ever be, regardless of how curious I was to explore that part of my sexuality with him.

"You're so beautiful," he said as he parted my legs. "Do you have any idea how lucky I feel to be married to you? To call you my lover?"

"Show me," I said.

When he started to enter me, he was so tender, it was if he was teasing me—which of course he was. With his thumb pressed firmly against my clit, he edged so gently into me that I had all I could do but to scream for him to take me.

"Do you want all of it?" he asked.

"Is that even a question?"

"What if I just tease you like this?" he said, nudging in and out of me without fully penetrating me. "Is that too much? Too little?" He pushed deeper inside of me, and then quickly withdrew so that the tip of his cock was throbbing against my clit. He allowed it to linger there for several unbearable moments before dipping his head down, taking my right nipple into his mouth, and flicking his tongue over it before doing the same to my left nipple. It made me want to crawl out of my body, onto the ceiling, and out one of the windows.

"Fuck me," I said.

"What kind of good Catholic girl speaks like that?" he asked.

"This one."

"You know, I could string you along like this all night if I wanted to."

"You heard what I said."

"And what if I didn't?"

"The hell you didn't. Fuck me."

And he did.

With one unexpected, brutal thrust, I felt the length of him fill me as my eyes adjusted just enough to the dim bedroom lighting so that I could see the love, the passion, and the fierceness on his face.

"That's right," I said as I hooked my legs around his ass, and urged him to drive even deeper into me. "That's how I want it—all of you. Every bit of you. But how long do you think you can keep that up without coming, Alex? Not long is my bet."

"Then get ready to lose that bet," he said as he pulled out of me—and then slammed so hard back into me that I threw back my head and gasped. "Because tonight is going to be another long night for you, my love. I'm going to ride you until you don't know where you are, what your name is, where you came from, what church you pray at, or where you even live."

I laughed when he said that—but it was a taunting laugh. "Please," I said. "You've got nothing—"

Before I could finish my sentence, he rammed into me and my words caught in my throat. I reached out my hands to cover his firm and lightly hairy pecs, and then I just gave myself over to him.

For the next hour, Alex kept me on the edge of climax. Whenever he sensed that I was close, he withdrew from me and brought his lips to my own as my climax subsided. It was torture, but in the best way that I could imagine.

Tonight, I clearly was to be played with. Throughout our lovemaking, Alex lifted me onto his lap, he fucked me on my side, he got me on my knees so he could come up behind me, and then, when it was clear that each of us was close, he flipped me around with the sort of effortless ease that reminded me just how strong he was.

As he pounded into me, my head lolled from side to side as I moved toward the bright edges of climax. With his lips on mine, I felt completely alive, as if my skin—which was as slick with sweat as his—was thrumming with a host of nerve endings I never knew existed.

"I'm going to come," I said.

"Then let me swallow it."

When he said that, he bucked even harder against me, and pressed his mouth even harder against mine. And when I did come, I let out a stifled scream that Alex took into himself just a moment before coming himself.

At that moment, I wasn't sure if we'd ever been one like this, which seemed crazy to me at this point in our relationship. But when our lips finally parted and we each gasped for air, I cupped my heavy breasts as the sensation subsided, and I stroked my fingers through his hair before he pulled out of me and lay down beside me.

With deft hands, he turned me so that my back faced him. And as he moved in close to me, his erection pulsed against my buttocks, and I said that I loved him.

"You're part of my soul," he said. "I hope that you know that, Jennifer, but I'm not sure that you know how deep it goes with me when it comes to you. Sometimes, it even surprises me, but I'm grateful for it and for you. I love that I'm able to call you my wife. My partner. My best friend. My lover."

"How are we ever going to go for four days without having sex?" I said to him. "Are there hotels nearby?"

"Babe, after last Christmas, don't you know me by now? You and I are good. I've already worked all of that shit out."

6

———

THE NEXT MORNING, all of the Christmas gifts I'd purchased with Blackwell's help—along with an alarming amount of wrapped packages that Alex had purchased on his own and somehow hidden from me in his office closet—were placed into the SUV Cutter was driving for us.

"We're going to need another car," I said to Cutter as the doormen placed my gifts next to the ones that Alex had bought himself. "As large as this SUV is, there's no way in hell that all of us are going to fit into it, especially since I know what Blackwell is bringing to the party."

"Look behind you," Cutter said. "Madison's former driver, Zack, is ready to follow us to Blackwell's apartment in that SUV, which seats eight."

"Thank you for that!" I said. "Because I'm telling you that I've already seen what Blackwell has purchased, and for that alone, we're going to need two rides to get to LaGuardia. And then there's Brock and Madison to consider," I said. "Who knows what they're bringing? We might need a third car."

"If we do, I can make that happen sooner than you

think," he said. "Don't worry about it because I already have another car on standby. So, let's go and pick up Brock and Madison, who stayed at the Plaza last night to make picking up everybody easier for us this morning. And then we'll pick up Blackwell and the girls."

WHEN WE ARRIVED at the Plaza, Brock and Madison were waiting in the lobby for us.

"We might have purchased a few things," Madison said to me.

She was wearing a fitted, gorgeous Alexander McQueen double-breasted textured rose coat in black, which I thought looked stunning on her. She also wore a pair of dark denim skinny jeans, and a black boot I could have sworn I saw at Prada. As for Brock, he was wearing a revealing pair of Selvedge straight-slim jeans and a Marc Jacobs Bane leather jacket in black, which matched his hair and beard. I thought that he looked hot—and that these two made for one handsome couple. They were young, urban, and clearly in love.

"It's nothing crazy, but we wanted to offer something," Brock said.

These two were still just getting started at Wenn. They were making a good salary and receiving quarterly performance bonuses. But still, despite how they were dressed now—which I imagined had everything to do with receiving Blackwell's approval and dodging that bullet should she fire it at them—they had to be living on a budget. Living in Manhattan was far from inexpensive.

"This is about spending time together," I said. "You didn't have to do anything."

"We wanted to," Madison said. She motioned behind

her at the bellman, who was standing beside a brass baggage cart stacked with presents. "It's not much, but it's what we could afford. I hope you understand."

I went over and gave her a hug as Alex shook his cousin's hand and then exchanged a few slaps on the back. "It's more than enough," I said. "Thank you both. Sincerely."

"I tried my best when it came to picking out the right thing for Blackwell, but I'm pretty certain that she's going to be underwhelmed by it. Brock and I would have loved to have bought her a new Birkin or a new Chanel suit, but that's just not in the cards for us right now."

"And she knows that," I said. "I'm sure that a lot of thought went into everything Brock and you chose, and that's what matters. But please don't stress out over any of it. These next few days aren't about the gifts, OK? They're meant to be fun. I can't have you thinking that you should have done more or less going into the holidays. This is purely about spending time with family and friends—and I mean that, Madison. You'll see. You and I, after all, have been elected to cook Christmas dinner!"

"We have?" she said. "Oh, I love to cook! Just ask Brock."

"She's an amazing cook," he said. "In fact, I've been hitting the gym hard because of her cooking."

"I'm so on board," Madison said to me. "We'll put on a feast."

"Indeed, we will," I said.

"We should go," Alex said. "Blackwell, Daniella, and Alexa are likely waiting for us—and we all know how that will go if we're even a minute late."

∽

SINCE BLACKWELL always carried with her a bag of demands, I was instructed to call her just before we arrived.

"We're here," I said as we pulled up in front of her Fifth Avenue apartment complex. "Are you ready to go?"

"Don't count on it," she said in a hushed voice. "Those two have been at it since morning."

"Over what?"

"Boy things. Apparently, Daniella has killed off yet another one."

"Another one? How many men can that girl go through in a year? Is she all right?"

"You know how she is. Whenever this happens to her, she becomes moody and difficult in an effort to conceal whatever hurt and disappointment she's feeling. And this time it must be significant, because that girl has been impossible. She and Alexa had a fight this morning that likely shook this city to its core. But enough about that. We'll be down in five minutes. Be prepared for their sour moods, and also for a motherlode of gifts. I'll need space for them. You did reserve space for me, didn't you?"

"We have a separate SUV to accommodate everything, so don't worry. I'll ride with you and the girls. Alex will ride with Cutter, Brock, and Madison. And because today I feel like nothing short of a Christmas angel, I'll also help you keep the peace between the girls."

"At this point and in their state right now, that's a long shot. What I really need is for you to become a member of the United Nations. You have no idea what those two have been like since they started in on each other this morning. It's been disastrous. But join me in keeping them at bay at your own peril! I'll see you in five."

But it was a full twenty minutes before Blackwell and the girls arrived—which was pushing it since we needed to board the Lear at 11:30, thirty minutes before our takeoff. With haste, Alex, Cutter, and Zack started to put all of Blackwell's gifts and luggage into the back of Zack's SUV, while I went over to hug Blackwell, and then Daniella and Alexa.

"How are you, girls?" I asked.

"At war," Alexa said.

"Please," Daniella said. "You're no longer worthy of my time. And neither is anyone else." She turned toward Cutter, who thankfully was out of earshot. "With the exception of Cutter."

"Oh, God, Daniella—not this again," Blackwell said.

"Oh, yes," Daniella said. "Just look at him—perfection. Still single, I assume? Don't bother answering, because I already know that he is. And how can that possibly even be the case? For reasons that I still can't wrap my head around, that bitch he was seeing dumped him in favor of moving forward with her career, as if that's the fucking meaning of life? Still, her loss is my gain. Just watch me win him over this time, because I plan to. After dear Susan's departure, Cutter must be longing for the right woman to come along. And I am *so* the right woman. I've said it time and again, but no one will listen to me. So listen up, kids, because their break up happened for a reason. The universe has spoken. It knows that we were meant to be together."

"What do you, of all people, know about the universe?" Alexa said. "Let alone our own planet, which is in its death throes at this point. Given the sheer amount of hairspray you used this morning, which knocked a few more holes into the ozone, it's clear that you don't give a shit about anything or anyone other than yourself. Your whole being is just about serving yourself. I think that you're a grotesque."

"And I think that you're just jelly because you'll never be

able to serve up the kind of hotness that I'm offering right now. I mean look at me, for God's sake. I'm totes turning it out—as I do every day."

"God, you're shallow. It hurts me to even call you my sister."

"I'm not shallow where it matters most," Daniella said.

"Which brings us back to the fact that you're also pretty much a bonafide slut."

"Says the dyke who hasn't even been laid yet—*even though you are in your twenties*. You're so pathetic, Alexa, it's embarrassing."

"I'm not a lesbian, Daniella. But if I were and if you had a problem with that, it would reveal who you really are at heart. A homophobe."

"Whatevs. I love the gays."

"That's enough!" Blackwell said through gritted teeth. "I told you to get in line, and I meant it. Don't cross me."

"I speak the truth, and your little tree-hugger here knows it, Mommie Dearest."

"Here's the truth," Alexa said. "The reason Cutter wants nothing to do with Daniella is because her self-esteem is so far in the gutter, she comes off as desperate. Needy. Wanton. Messy. Why would any man like him, who totally has his shit together, ever be interested in someone like her? Here's a quick answer—he wouldn't. So, Daniella, don't get your hopes up when it comes to Cutter—because he likely sees you as poison, just as the rest of us do."

LATER, when we finally were in the air and headed toward Maine, I asked Madison to join me in the galley and took her aside.

"So," I said, discreetly nodding over toward Daniella and Alexa, who were sitting well away from each other. "Have you sensed the tension between those two?"

"You mean in ways that might have rocketed the planet off its normal trajectory?"

"How about if we try to quell it?"

"With a nuclear bomb?"

"No, but close to one. Look, I know that it's only noon, but we now are officially on vacation. Even though it's only an hour's flight from here to Bangor, what do you say we haul out the drink cart and try to make things festive?"

"That could go one of two ways," she said. "If those two get lit, tensions could explode. But if they just get a happy little buzz, maybe it'll help them get along. You know them far better than I do, so what's your take?"

"At their cores, they actually love each other. I've seen it first-hand in ways that I won't bore you with now. But it's real—there is love between them, as impossible as that is for you to fathom right now. And trust me—I've actually seen how the help of one drink can actually lighten their moods. That said, any more than one drink would indeed be a complete disaster, so we need to keep this just to the one."

"Then I say it's drinks for everyone!" she said.

We were flying without a flight attendant because Cutter was trained to handle any kind of air emergency, so Madison and I loaded up the cart with fresh ice, clean glasses, napkins, and bottles of booze. When we were finished, we winked at each other, and then entered the cabin.

"Drinks, anyone?" I called out as I pressed the silver cart in front of me.

"Oh, no you're not," Alex said.

"Oh, yes I am," I said. "This party has officially begun.

Who wants what? Madison and I have a bit of everything—
even a Guinness for you, Cutter, because Tank told me that's
what you drink."

"He and I love our Guinness," he said. "But I'm on duty,
Jennifer, so I'll need to pass."

"And I appreciate that," I said. "But how about if you just
take one sip when we all toast each other? Certainly that
won't hurt. What do you think?"

"One sip should be fine," he said. "But just one.
I'm game."

"Groovy!"

"Who in the hell says 'groovy'?" I heard Daniella say
under her breath. "I thought Jennifer was cooler than that."

"Shut up, Daniella," Alexa said. "You're being rude."

"Whatevs. When it comes to my Jenny from the block, I
expect more than that kind of shit."

I saw that Alexa was about to speak back to her sister
when Cutter said, "Criticizing our hosts on any level seems
disrespectful to me. Wouldn't you agree, Daniella?"

Shit just got real!

"Oh," she said as she looked across the aisle at him. "I
was only joking."

"The hell you were," Alexa said.

"No, I was. I love the word 'groovy.' I really do. And I
know she only said it in jest. I'm grateful to Alex and to
Jennifer for inviting us along. And I'm especially grateful
that *you're* here, Cutter."

He didn't respond to that. Instead, he just took the glass
of Guinness I offered to him and sat still in silence while
Daniella blinked at him and Madison and I moved down
the aisle to serve drinks to everyone.

7

WHEN WE ARRIVED at the cabin Alex had rented for us, the use of the word 'cabin' no longer held any meaning for us. Seeing photographs of this beast of a house was one thing. But driving up to it in person? That was an experience that even I didn't expect. This place was pretty much a snow-bound mansion.

"Oh, my God," I said as we approached it. "Look at it Barbara—it's amazing."

"Well, it certainly is large," she said. "And I have to admit that it's lovely. Look at all of the floor-to-ceiling windows. And how they've lit the whole house from within in anticipation of our arrival. Gorgeous. And look at the lake to our left, which is stunning, even in twilight. How big is this house again?"

"Something like nine-thousand square feet, I think. Maybe more—I can't quite remember. But it's huge."

"It should offer all of us plenty of room."

"To say the least. Alex went out of his way to take care of all of us, which just makes me love him more. And look at how private it is. I don't see another house in sight."

"Neither do I, so I'm declaring this as nothing short of a goddamned snow-globe miracle," Blackwell said as we arrived at the estate. "In fact, as I look at it, I can actually imagine this house tucked into one of those ridiculous, touristy little snow globes. Shake the damned thing, and watch the snow fall down upon it like diamonds. That said, I can only hope that the inside matches the outside, because one never knows..."

"I've seen the photos," I said. "I think that we'll be fine, but we'll see. What do you think, girls?"

"All I need is my own bedroom and bathroom, and I'm good," Daniella said. "But it is beautiful," she added. "Where is Cutter going to sleep?"

Neither Blackwell nor I answered that question, even though we both knew that wherever he slept, it would be far away from her.

"Is it solar powered?" Alexa asked. "Because with a bright blue sky and all of the snow surrounding it, just imagine what solar energy could do for a house such as this. I'll love it even more if I find out that it uses green energy. But even if it doesn't, Jennifer, it's amazing. Thank you for inviting us. I mean, look at that lake! It's like the ocean. I can't see an end to it. I so want to explore it, along with the woods. And to breathe in the fresh air. To hear the sounds of birds I've never heard before. And maybe we'll even see deer. Or moose. Or whatever! I'm really excited."

"What you need to come face-to-face with is a skunk," Daniella said. "Or better yet—a bear. Because all of this mooning of yours over nature makes me want to vomit. What I want to know is this—how close are we to the bars? Where are the best restaurants? Because if Cutter decides he really does want nothing to do with me, I want to know where I need to go to find men who are single and available.

I already know that this place is loaded with them. People come to ski resorts for two simple reasons—to ski and to get laid. I'm here for the latter."

"You're such a whore," Alexa said.

"And a satisfied one."

"Who are you?" Blackwell said. "Where did I go wrong with you to make you speak like that?"

"I'm a grown woman, Mother. I make my own decisions when it comes to my body. And after the way Cutter shut me down on the plane, I'm prepared to move on—if I need to, not that I'm counting that out just yet. But if that turns out to be the case, my body is needing me some big, strapping, ski-sloping stud to come along as soon as possible. Before I leave here, somebody's jingle bells will be banging against my doorbell. I can promise all of you that."

"You're disgusting," Alexa said.

"And you should turn yourself over to the Amish," Daniella said. "You are so repressed, my little lesbo virgin. And how sad is that?"

"Oh, Daniella," Alexa said. "How I want to cry for you right now. What you don't know is that when it comes to this trip? I'm about to put your sorry ass to shame."

"What the hell does that even mean?"

"Nothing," Alexa said. "Or everything. We'll see."

When she said that, there was a light, teasing, lilting tone to her voice, which no one could overlook—nor its implications.

What does *she have up her sleeve?*

"Anyway," I intervened in a light voice that sounded canned even to me as the SUV pulled in front of the house. "We're here! So, let's get out of the car and explore."

~

THE HOUSE WAS beyond any of our expectations.

As Cutter moved all of our luggage and gifts out of the SUVs and into the foyer, the lot of us just looked around when we stepped inside.

"It's fantastic," I said as I wrapped my arm around Alex's waist. "It's perfect, Alex!"

"I'm glad that you like it, Mrs. Wenn."

"And I do, Mr. Wenn. Just look at this place! And look into the living room at the tree—how tall is that thing? Twenty feet? It must be. And look at the decorations— they're beautiful," I said. "It's beyond what I'd imagined, Alex. Thank you!"

"It's my pleasure," he said. "I had nothing to do with the tree or with the decorating, though from what I can see, the team I hired did a fine job. When it comes to these sorts of rentals, you never really know what you're getting into. But a friend of mine recommended this place to me, so on his advice alone, I went with it. And he was right. So far, this place looks great, and we've yet to see all of it."

"Where are the bedrooms?" Daniella asked. "I want to choose mine before anyone else chooses theirs."

"The bedrooms have already been assigned," Alex said.

"They've been what?"

"Just what I said. Jennifer and I have ours. Brock and Madison have theirs. And your mother, Cutter, you, and Alexa each have your own. There is no picking or choosing when it comes to who wants which room, so my suggestion is that you enjoy what you have, and be happy that you have it. I doubt that you'll be disappointed."

"But what if I am?" she said.

And when Daniella said that, Alex stepped away from me and walked over to her.

"Then I'd be pleased to put you back on a plane back to

Manhattan, Daniella. I'm not joking, because you're an adult now, and at this point in your life, you know how to behave —especially when you're a guest. After last Christmas, I expect you to be on your best behavior while we're here. And believe me—I mean that."

"Oh, burn!" Alexa said.

"I don't need your help, Alexa," he said. "Because I also expect the same from you while we're here. No bickering or fighting between you two. I won't have it."

"That's right," Daniella said. "Because she's the one who always starts it."

"That's not true," Alexa said. "You do."

"Enough," Alex said.

"Agreed," Blackwell said.

"You are our guests. We've gone to a great deal of trouble to make this Christmas something memorable for everyone. And I hope that both of you will appreciate your good fortune because of our efforts. But that's up to you two. If you find that you can't be polite to each other, then I'll send you back to Manhattan, and next year we'll reassess whether you'll be invited to join us again."

"Well, that's kind of harsh," Daniella said.

"Actually, he's right," Alexa said. "Uncle Alex, I promise that I'll keep myself in check even if she doesn't."

"You're such a suck-up, Alexa. You always have been."

"All right," Alex said. "So, right now I'm going to just address you, Daniella. You just turned twenty-three. And in my opinion? It's time for you to act like it. Our time here means too much to me and to everyone else for you to ruin it for us. And I'm telling you right now that I won't allow you to ruin it. Am I clear on that?"

"Uncle Alex—"

"There's nothing more to say on the matter, Daniella.

Either you agree, or you disagree. You're no longer a little girl—and you haven't been one for some time. So that pass I gave you when you were acting up last Christmas is long gone at this point. At your age, you know how to treat people with respect. You also need to know that there are consequences if you don't."

"I've been going through a difficult time," she said. "I got dumped by another guy last week!"

"And why do you think that is?" Alex asked.

Before she could answer, he pressed on.

"We all go through difficult times, Daniella, but that doesn't mean that we should take it out on those who love us. Do you understand that? I'm not sure that you do. In fact, I think that you've become so spoiled since your parents got divorced, you take everything that comes your way for granted—as if you deserve what is being offered to you. But here's the thing—you don't deserve any of it. Instead, you're just lucky to have access to it. You are surrounded by people who love you, and yet you somehow just push people's buttons with a kind of ugliness that I've never seen before."

"Ugliness?"

"Yes, ugliness. And believe me—I've seen plenty of ugliness during my lifetime, especially as Wenn's CEO. So, I'm going to be straight with you right now—all of your bad behavior ends here. If you don't want to comply, you can leave. No hard feelings—just go. I'll have a plane ready to take you back to New York within a matter of hours, and you can either spend the holidays alone in Manhattan, or with your friends. Whatever you wish. At this point and given your behavior, I can honestly say that I don't care. So, it's your call whether you stay or go, and also whether you turn yourself around when it comes to how you treat people. So, decide."

"Oh, my," Blackwell said in a voice so low that only I could hear it.

"I don't mean to be difficult," she said.

"I think that you do, if only for the attention you receive. And look at how that's turned out for you—me, of all people, actually asking you to leave if you don't agree to shape up. That's something I never thought I'd have to do, but I will do what's right to make certain that the rest of us have a pleasant holiday, because after this year? We deserve one. It's in your hands, Daniella. Decide."

"I want to be with all of you," she said. "I've just had a hard year."

"And you think that those around you haven't? After the year we've just gone through? Cutter almost died, for God's sake. Have you forgotten that? So did your sister—have you forgotten that as well?"

"I stayed by my sister's side throughout everything she went through on that island. You know that."

"Then where is that person now?"

And when he said that, she just looked at Alex, clearly at a loss for words.

"I saw how you cared for Alexa after she was bitten. I also saw how you cared for Cutter. And because of that, I know that you have it within you to be a decent person. But that person often goes missing when it comes to you, Daniella, and you need to face that fact and grow up because of it. You need to be kind. You need to be humble. You need to know that this house—this holiday—is not owed to you just because you're associated with me. We've come here to celebrate the holidays, not to let your ridiculous tantrums ruin them. So, why don't we just end this right here—do you want to celebrate the holiday with us, or not?"

"Of course I do."

"Well, that's good, because all of us want you here."

"I don't," Alexa said.

"That's enough, Alexa," Alex said.

"Sorry."

He turned back to Daniella. "I need to know if you understand my position on this."

"I do."

"Do you agree to stay given the conditions I've set out for you?"

"I can try. You know how I am, Uncle Alex. I can't promise that I'll be perfect—that would just be a lie. But I'll try my best to dial it down a notch."

"Several notches."

"OK, several notches."

"Now give me a hug."

And when she did, I saw on Daniella's face the sensitive girl behind the angry façade. For whatever reason, her self-esteem was so low that it revealed itself in ways that were cutting and sometimes awful. But beneath it all, I knew that deep within her was a good person. She just needed to believe that herself.

"Now, give your sister a hug," Alex said when they parted.

"I have to hug the anti-Christ?"

"She's not the anti-Christ. Hug her."

"Oh, Christ." She turned to Alexa, and when she did, I saw that her eyes were bright with tears. "All right—fine. Give me a hug."

"Are you carrying any sharp objects on you?" Alexa asked before they touched. "You know—like a knife? A sword? Because my back would like to know."

"Just my tongue, but that's in check. You're safe."

"Fine then—let's hug it out."

And they did. And when they did, I reached down and took Blackwell's hand in my own, which she squeezed at once. I knew that the exchange between Alex and Daniella hadn't been easy for her to hear, but I also knew Blackwell well enough to know that she believed that what he had said to her was for the best.

On some profound level, Daniella hated herself. But why? Was it because of her parents' divorce? Did she feel somehow responsible for that? It was possible—often, the children of divorce blamed themselves for the divorce. Or was it for a reason that none of us knew? What would it take for Daniella to decide that she could love herself? And in the process, love others as well?

Because when she realized that she could and that she should, I knew in my heart that that girl could turn her life around.

8

AFTER THE TENSE EXCHANGE, which led to Daniella apologizing to her mother for 'being such a bitch most of the time,' the mood lifted. People seemed to let out a collective sigh of relief, and we toured the rest of the house together.

Moving from room to room, we all first stopped short when we came upon the kitchen, which was so large and so beautiful, it seemed otherworldly, and then we went to the living room, the media room, the sauna, the sweeping room that housed the huge indoor pool and bubbling Jacuzzi, and finally to all of our bedrooms.

When the tour was over, all of us retreated to our bedrooms so that we could unpack. We were hungry, after all. It was time to get dressed, get ourselves to a restaurant of some sort, and enjoy a good meal before we hit the slopes the next day.

"You were amazing," I said to Alex when we were alone. "I know what you said to Daniella couldn't have been easy for you, but I think that what you said did a great deal of good for her. For some reason, that girl is hurting. There's got to be a reason behind why she behaves so poorly. You couldn't see the look on her face when you hugged her, but I did, and to me, it looked as if she was about to cry. It was as if you recognized some part of her that she hated about herself, and making it public seemed to me like it was some kind of a relief to her."

"It's time for her to grow up, Jennifer. Enough of her bickering bullshit."

"I couldn't agree more. But enough of that. Do you know where you'd like to eat tonight, or should I call ahead somewhere and make a reservation for us?"

"We're eating here," he said.

"We're eating here? Who's cooking? Me? Why didn't you tell me?"

He came over and wrapped his arms around my waist. "I'd never spring something like that on you," he said after he kissed me.

"Then how are we eating here? Take out?"

"On our first night here, I thought that it would be nice if we ate in. You saw how the dining room overlooks the lake and looks into the living room, where the lighted Christmas tree stands. And my SlimPhone has told me that tonight there will be a full moon hovering over that lake. I asked Ann to assemble a team of local chefs to cook dinner for us, and though you can't hear them now because this house is so damned big, they should already be in the kitchen preparing dinner as we speak."

"You gave them a key?"

"Ann gave them the code to enter the house. We'll have drinks and appetizers first in the living room, and then we'll have dinner. Tomorrow, we'll ski—and since we'll all need a good night's sleep for that, I thought that this would be a better solution than taking the time to get dressed up and going out. We're tired at this point. So, I figured that it was best to make tonight easier on us."

"Do you know how much I love you?" I asked.

"I'm pretty sure that I do, but I never tire of hearing it."

"How about if I just show you? I love you this much," I said as I kissed him meaningfully on the lips. "And if we had time before dinner, I'd show you in other ways."

"Maybe after dinner?"

"Bank on it," I said. And the moment I said that, I tossed myself into his arms, we fell onto our ridiculously oversized bed, and I smothered him with a blizzard of kisses that would rival any blizzard we might find tomorrow on the slopes.

WE JOINED the others for drinks and hors d'oeuvres in the living room next to the towering, fresh-smelling Christmas tree, beneath which the staff had already tucked the gifts. The colors of the packages, along with the ribbons attached to them, looked gorgeous to me.

In the massive fireplace to the tree's right, a fire flickered, crackled, and spat; classic Christmas music filled the space from the surround-sound speakers; and the servers Alex had hired delighted us with platters of scallops wrapped in bacon, oyster tartlets, buckwheat-cheddar blinis with smoked salmon, pancetta-wrapped mushrooms, cheddar gougères, and best of all, roasted shrimp with a garlic dipping sauce, which for me was the highlight.

Despite Alex's confrontation with Daniella, the mood was surprisingly festive and bright, likely because Alexa hadn't arrived yet. God only knew what would occur when she decided to join the party. But for now, people were happily mixing and chatting.

Brock and Madison were so close, they literally were hand-in-hand. Blackwell was rocking it in a bright red Chanel suit with black piping that accompanied her black pumps. Daniella herself was wearing a little black dress that I thought looked adorable on her, especially since she'd swept her hair away from her face in a low ponytail that revealed just how pretty she was. Her makeup was fresh and light, and she looked beautiful.

And then Alexa joined the room—and when she did, it was as if all of the oxygen had been sucked out of it. All heads turned to her.

"Sorry I'm late," she said as she walked toward us with a confidence I'd never seen in her before. "Can I have a martini? Dirty? Three olives?"

"Of course you can," I said as I went over to hug her. "Alexa, you look amazing!"

"That was the intent."

Clearly, it was—and she'd stolen the show because of it. She was wearing something that daring—a shimmering pair of skinny black slacks, black slingbacks with a three-inch heel, and to cover her otherwise naked torso, nothing more than a sequined black vest, which revealed more of her body than I'd ever seen before. Alexa generally wore baggy, unremarkable clothing, so I certainly didn't know that she sported *that* kind of a banging body—but she did, and she was owning it now.

She was a knock-out. With her face fully made up, including a bold red lip and a smoky eye, and with her dark hair scraped away from her face with the assistance of some sort of gel that made it glisten in the warm light, she looked sexy and stunning in ways that I knew were intentional.

She'd come here to put her sister to shame—and even though I didn't want to take sides, it already was clear to me, and likely to everyone else in the room, that Alexa was the standout.

In her own scathing way, Daniella had always referred to Alexa as some sort of stereotypical hippie or lesbian. But whatever her sexuality was—not that I gave a damn about it —tonight she looked to me like some sort of seductress from a James Bond movie.

She was that hot.

"What in the fresh hell has happened to you?" Blackwell said.

"I'm sorry," Alexa said as one of the servers brought her a martini. She lifted it to the group, took a sip after everyone had lifted their drink to hers, and then turned her glance to her mother. "What are you referring to?"

"You know damned well what I'm referring to."

"It's just a look, Mother."

"And since you're my daughter, you know how powerful a 'look' can be. When did you come up with this? I love it! The shoes, the hair, the makeup—it's so sophisticated, it's beyond divoon. I always knew you had this in you. So, let's just consider this your Christmas present to me delivered a few days early."

"She's outdone all of us!" Daniella cried out in despair. "How can that even be?!"

"It's a reality, Daniella," Alexa said. "In this case, because of the assistance of Tom Ford, whom I'm wearing tonight. And this is far from the end of it, because I've prepared for this holiday in ways that even you can't fathom. If you think that this is all I've got, I'm here to tell you that this is the least of what I've got. So, you know, I hope you packed well, because I know for a fact that *I* did. And what I'm about to bring to the game this holiday weekend is going to shut you down for years to come. Just watch me. Whether we're on the slopes or off for a night at the bars, I plan to bring it—in ways that are going to crush you."

"No, you won't."

"Just watch me." She took another sip of her martini and eyed Daniella's dress. "By the way—cute look. I could see you showing up like that at a parent-teacher conference."

"Oh, it's so game on!" Daniella said.

"It is," Alexa agreed calmly. "And do you want to know why? Obviously, you don't—your heated glare already is telling me a solid 'no.' So, I'll nevertheless give you an insider's glimpse. Here's what I know about you, Daniella. I helped you pack before we left. Do you remember how helpful I was? How attentive I was? What a good sister I was? And do you even know the reason why I bothered to help you? Probably not, because I'll outsmart you every time. I was helpful because I wanted to see what you were bringing with you, and once I knew what that was? I went on a shopping spree in an effort to beat your ass—and I succeeded. Call it sabotage. Call it a knife in your back. Hell, call it what you will. But while I'm here in Maine? I'm the one who's going to get the boys. Just watch me, sweet pea— because all of that is about to come my way in ways that you've never seen before. What I'm wearing alone should shut down your constant questions about my sexuality, which I'm tired of hearing at this point. I'm going to get properly shagged while we're here. The question is whether you will..."

9

THE NEXT MORNING, after a tense evening that eventually evened itself out—if only because of the great food and booze—it was going to be off to the slopes for all of us, and it was the perfect day for it. Bright and sunny, and not unreasonably cold. When I checked the temperature on my SlimPhone, it said that it was nineteen degrees outside. I'd certainly seen far worse than that during my years growing up in Maine—and *that* temperature was perfectly tolerable when it came to skiing.

Alex wasn't in bed when I woke up, so I assumed that he was already in the shower, but when I checked the adjoining bathroom, he wasn't there either.

Where is he?

Since it was only five o'clock, I didn't call out for him because I didn't want to wake anybody. Instead, I put on a silky red robe over my red negligee, and started to move through the house looking for him, only stopping when I heard sounds coming from the kitchen. As I passed the dining room, I saw that it was already set with new linens and tableware, and when I crossed into the kitchen, there was Alex, apparently preparing breakfast.

"What are you doing?" I said in a low voice when I entered the room. He was wearing a tantalizing pair of black, slim-fit stretch jogging pants that hugged his ass in ways that made me want to spank it and a grey, long-sleeved jersey tee that stretched across his broad chest. His hair was tousled in ways that made me want to haul him back to the bedroom so that I could have my way with him. Who needed breakfast when I had the breakfast of champions right here in front of me?

"Making breakfast for all of us," he said.

"For all of us? How long have you been up?"

"Since four."

"Why didn't you ask me to help you? How in the hell do you plan to feed all of us on your own? There are eight of us, for God's sake. You should have woken me. We could have done this together."

"I wanted to do this on my own," he said. "Spending money is easy for me, Jennifer. But putting on a great breakfast for everyone takes an effort, and that effort means something that money can't buy. And don't forget that I learned to cook from a master."

"Michelle," I said. "Your parents' cook. You loved her."

"She took me under her wing, taught me how to cook, and in the process, she helped me to escape from my parents."

"What are you making? It smells delicious."

"Exactly what Michelle used to make whenever my parents entertained a crowd—potato basil frittatas. Four of them. They're already in the oven, along with the bacon. Did you know that it's best to cook bacon in the oven?"

"I've never heard of that."

"It's the easiest way to cook it. No splattering. No grease. And when you put them on a rack, they come out straight—not wrinkled. I have coffee ready to go when it's time to get that cranking, and I'll admit that I have three cheats."

"Which are?"

"Freshly squeezed orange juice, home-churned butter, and croissants. Ann made a few calls for me before we left Manhattan. She found a local caterer who does all of her own cooking, and she contacted her for me. Betty came this morning with three jugs of juice, the butter she makes herself from her own cows, and two dozen croissants that came out of the oven just about an hour ago. Can you smell them?"

"I can smell everything—and it smells amazing."

He smiled when I said that—and the dimples I loved so much only deepened in his cheeks. "I set the table after I made the frittatas—and at this point, everything is ready to go. It wasn't difficult. Breakfast will be served in one hour, and since we're hitting the slopes today, it's a total power breakfast. Plenty of protein. We're going to rock that mountain. Even Blackwell. Because of this breakfast alone, she's going to nail those bunny slopes."

"From your lips to God's ears."

"That's an interesting way to put it. How about if your lips were on mine right now?"

I didn't hesitate, and when our lips met, I felt a longing to be with Alex but I knew with a clear sense of disappointment that I couldn't be.

"How are we going to get through these next few days without being intimate with each other?" I said. "I don't want to hold back. Last year, we went to a no-tell motel for just that reason. There must be a hotel nearby. Can we go to it?"

"Unnecessary," he said.

"What does that mean?"

"Have you even seen the size of this house?" he asked. "And how I made certain when I rented it that the master bedroom was far away from the other bedrooms? Jennifer, I have this covered. Nobody will be able to hear us. Trust me on that."

10

AFTER BREAKFAST, which was a roaring success due to Alex's excellent skills in the kitchen and because everyone seemed rested and ready for the day, we retired to our bedrooms, suited up, and then met in the living room to depart for the slopes.

And that's where everything went wrong.

"While I love Chanel," Blackwell said when she stepped into the room in her new suit, "I'm certainly not sure about *this* look. Look at me, for God's sake. I look like a goddamned tampon—and one that has been used! This red is nothing short of the color of blood."

"Oh, it is not," I said. "You look fab. And it's Chanel. I actually think that you look not only stylish, but hot. And please, all of us know that no one is going to be wearing anything even remotely close to *that* on the slopes."

"And for good reason. I haven't had a period in four years—and look at me. Aunt Flow is back. I might as well be a walking advertisement for planned parenthood."

"Seriously?" Daniella said.

"Seriously," Blackwell countered.

"Mom, you look fantastic."

"You're just fishing for one of my credit cards."

"No, I'm not—you look great."

"You do," Madison said.

"And you're just digging for another promotion."

"She is not," Brock said. "Because you do look great."

"I remain unconvinced."

Did she really dislike the suit, or was she just creating a moment of drama because she was Blackwell? I could never be sure when it came to her. "But Madison and I thought that you loved the suit..."

"Look, it will do," she said, holding up her Chanel goggles and placing them on her face. "Especially since I can hide behind these. But you have to admit that this particular shade of red *is* the color of blood. If Alexa would hurry up, get dressed, and get her ass down here, she'd tell me that all of this was a sign from the universe. And that the moment I take to those slopes, *I'll* be the one who's going to be covered in blood. If that's the case, I want no part of this."

"You are going to be fine," Cutter said.

"Says the ex-Navy SEAL who already has been boasting about his skiing abilities."

"Jennifer and I are going to ski alongside you. I've already looked at all of the trails online, and the easiest one is called 'the Birches'. It's designed for beginners. I also checked out a few videos of it online, and even young children were conquering it with ease. It's a very gentle slope. Will it take you a bit to learn how to ski? Yes. But once you learn a few tricks that Jennifer and I will show you, I think you'll find out that it's easy and fun."

"And if you get hungry, you can eat some snow," Madison said. "The alternative to ice!"

"Oh, aren't you clever," she said. "Beware of my wrath,

girl." She turned to Alex, who, like Brock and Cutter, was wearing a snug-fitting black ski suit that hugged his ass in ways that I thought were rather appealing. "What about you?" she said. "You're awfully quiet. What do you think about this?"

"Your suit, or the drama you're creating?"

"How cheeky of you. How quick. How off the hip. Naturally, the former."

"I agree with the others."

"Well, then it's done," she said. "I'll carry on looking like a goddamned blood bank—and in the meantime, I plan on beating those slopes."

"That's the spirit," Alex said. "Remember, we're here to have fun."

"I don't even know what that is."

"Why do I believe that?"

"Because you've known me since you were a child?"

"Anyway," he said, "how about if we remind you what fun is?"

"At the potential of risking my own life? Why not? But I will tell all of you this—that mountain isn't going to beat me. I can promise all of you that."

"I totes see you slamming head-on into a tree," Daniella said. "And that's why I'm skiing with you, Jennifer, and Cutter. If you think I'm going to miss this shit, you've got another thing coming."

At that moment, Alexa walked into the room.

"Sorry to be late," she said.

When everyone turned to face her, Daniella's breath was the first to catch in her throat, followed by Blackwell, who lifted her goggles and covered her mouth with the back of her hand.

And it was clear why she did.

Alexa was wearing a white-and-black Fendi fur collar ski jacket that I'd considered buying myself before we left, so I knew it had cost over five grand. It was fitted to her body and it was beyond chic, as were her black, slim-fitting Fendi ski pants, which revealed her curves in ways that I was still getting used to since she'd only first revealed them to us last night. A white headband held her dark hair back, and she wore just enough makeup to make her face look fresh.

"Alexa," I said. "What are you doing to us? You look lovely!"

"Thank you, Jennifer. But just so all of you know, I haven't sold out, nor will I ever sell out. The fur is faux and I'm wearing a cashmere roll neck jumper beneath my jacket, which is made of natural materials, as is the rest of my outfit."

"And which, by the way, has 'Fendi' spelled out in massive letters on your damned left arm," Daniella said. "When you entered your hippie phase a couple of years ago, you said that you were 'beyond labels.' That 'labels didn't define' you. And yet here you are now—a walking label. You're a fraud."

"Actually, I'm evolving."

"Whatevs."

"I think she looks great," Cutter said.

And when he said that, Daniella just looked at him. "Seriously?"

"I do. She does."

"What about me? Don't I look great? I'm wearing a damned Sonya Chodry Anya ski jacket with a Rex rabbit fur collar for God's sake. Do you have any idea what that cost my mother? Or the time I spent making myself up for you— I mean, for today," she said, quickly correcting herself, though entirely too late. "Because I can tell you this, Cutter —I put some serious effort into this."

"That's too bad," Alexa said. "I barely put any effort into what I'm wearing."

"The hell you didn't—you're late for a reason. You've probably been in that bathroom trying to figure out how to put on makeup. That's what took you so long."

"Sorry, but all I'm wearing is a light foundation from Aveda and a bit of mascara. That's it. Nothing more."

"Who are you?" Blackwell said.

"How many times are you going to ask me that?"

"Until it makes sense."

"I'm your daughter. And by the way, Mom, love the suit."

"You're unrecognizable to me."

"Just to reassure you, you did give birth to me. And, you know, also to the demon spawn turning bright red over there."

"Whatevs, Alexa."

"I'll second that." She clapped her hands. "So," Alexa said. "Shall we ski? Because I'm ready to rock the slopes!"

11

SINCE WE WERE RENTING our ski equipment at the lodge, all of us were able to fit into one of the massive black SUVs Alex had rented for us. Cutter drove. Alex sat next to him. Blackwell and the girls were in the second row, and I sat in the back with Brock and Madison because I wanted to spend some time with them.

"You look pretty sweet," I said to Madison. "I love your blue coat—it looks so warm. Where did you get it?"

"Macy's," she said in a voice so low only Brock and I could hear it. "And thanks for the compliment, Jennifer—but I'm here to tell you that this is far from Fendi. Or Sonya Chodry, for that matter—whoever she is. I just can't compete with any that."

"There is no competition taking place here," I said—and then I checked myself. "Well, that's not really true, is it? Clearly there's one going on between Alexa and Daniella right now, but that's their issue, not ours. And I really don't care to even discuss it. Those girls are lucky to have what they have. I grew up poor. So did you. Whenever I hear them behaving like that, I just want to scream. But I don't because I know that it will only make matters worse."

"I've only just met them," Madison said. "But five grand for a ski jacket? Seriously? I can't even wrap my head around the idea of spending that kind of money. But I have to say that it is cutting-edge. I mean, talk about style," she said. "But frankly, it *should* be stylish for that price."

When she said that, I saw Brock reach over and squeeze her hand. And that touched me. They were young and in love, and it emanated off them in ways that were palpable. For a moment, I recalled what it had felt like when I'd first decided to give my heart over to Alex—it had been terrifying, exhilarating, humbling and profound. Just looking at Brock and Madison now, I knew that on some level, they were feeling what I had felt when I first fell in love with the love of my life.

"How about you, Brock?" I asked. "It's been so insane since we got here, we haven't had much time to chat. Are you enjoying yourself?"

"What Alex and you have done for all of us is beyond gracious," he said. "I can't thank each of you enough. I mean, look at today's breakfast alone—it was amazing, and Alex got up early to do that for all of us. That's the cousin I love and remember."

"You're right," I said. "That's Alex—just one of the many reasons why I love and adore him."

"It's also one of the reasons why I'm grateful that we're closer now than we've been in years. He's always been ridiculously generous. I haven't had a family for a long time, Jennifer, but I feel as if I'm part of one now. I can't tell you what that means to me. If you knew my parents, I think you'd understand what this means to me." He furrowed his brow at me. "I have told you about my history with my parents, haven't I?"

"You have. Several years ago, you decided to separate yourself from them."

"I had no choice. My father is and always will be overbearing. He was trying to control my life so that it would mirror his own life. And because of that, I knew that I needed to make it on my own, so I put myself through Wharton without his help. And then Alex decided to give me a shot and offered me a job at Wenn. I want Alex and you to always know just how much it means to me that you've given me a chance."

"Maybe we should be thanking you, Brock. I believe it was you who nailed down five acquisitions for Wenn over the past six months that will net us hundreds of millions in profits. You did the research and made the recommendations to go after those companies, and just look at how well we'll prosper because of your efforts. Don't ever think that Alex or I believe that you coming to Wenn has been anything less than a gift, just as it has been with Madison."

"I appreciate that," he said.

"So do I," Madison said. "You have no idea."

"What both of you always need to know is that we're lucky to have you. But enough talk about business—let's move on. Who's skiing with whom?"

"Well, since this is Blackwell's first time on the slopes, I think that Madison and I will be skiing with you," Brock said. "We decided this morning that we kind of need to see what comes of that. Where is Alexa going?"

"She hasn't said yet. Let me ask." I leaned forward. "Alexa," I said.

She turned around and looked at me.

"Which team are you skiing with today?"

"Oh, come on. Do you really think that I'm going to miss out on my mother tackling these slopes? I'm with you, Cutter, and Daniella. I skied throughout college, so I think at the very least that all of us can help Mom."

"I don't need your help," Blackwell said. "Because I've done my own research before we even came here. I have watched a wealth of training videos on UsTube."

"That would be 'YouTube,' Mom," Alexa said.

"Whatever. Just know that I've seen enough to know how to ski properly. It can't be that difficult. Mere children were mastering those bunny slopes. So, bring it on," she said.

And when she said that, I heard Madison say beneath her breath, "Oh, dear..."

"Oh, dear, what?" Blackwell said.

But before Madison could answer her, Alexa interrupted. "Skiing isn't all that easy, Mom. I mean no disrespect, but you need to get your legs beneath you before you tackle even something as simple as the bunny slopes. We'll show you a few tricks before we go down the mountain. You know, things like how you can slow yourself down simply by turning your skis inward. When it's best to cut from left to right. That sort of thing."

"The bunny slopes," she said. "Ha! They have nothing on me. You'll see. I will claim them for my own."

"Alrighty, then. Does everyone have their cell phones on them?" Alexa asked.

Everyone did.

"Good," she said. "Because we're all going to need to have access to a phone in case we need an ambulance. When it comes to my mother, I think we all know that she's sometimes a little too confident for her own good, and in this case, that might not be a good thing."

"The hell it won't."

"That's fine," Alexa said. "And I like your confidence. But I still think that you're about to get schooled."

12

————

THE WHIFFLETREE CHAIR lift is a four-passenger, high-speed quad design that was manufactured to lift its patrons 1,100 feet to the top of the mountain. It is located on the mountain's east side, which Blackwell, Daniella, Alexa, Cutter, Brock, Madison, and I moved toward after we'd been fitted with our gear and had said our farewells to Alex, who wanted to take one of the mountain's more challenging trails.

"These skis," Blackwell said as she slid unsteadily along the flat, snowy grounds that led to the lifts. "Already, I can appreciate them. When you think about it, with these on my feet? It's as if I'm a goddamned supermodel in one of Uncle Karl's runway shows and that I'm simply sporting a ridiculous pair of five-inch heels. Naturally, I can do this. Obviously, I was born to do this. I just need to put my poles in the snow like this—and look at me! Off I go!"

"Oh, this is so not going to end well," I said to Madison.

"I think she might be a little over-confident..."

"When isn't she?"

"Come on," Blackwell called out to all of us as we trailed

after her. "I'm not going to freeze my ass off out here all day. Let's move it!"

Perhaps because of the pending holiday, the lines to board the lift were practically nonexistent. With Christmas so close, it was as if we had the mountain to ourselves. In this case, that meant about a five-minute wait to get onto one of the lifts. From my college days alone with Lisa, I could remember coming here and waiting at least thirty minutes for a lift. A five-minute wait was unheard of to me.

"Barbara," Cutter said. "This is what I need you to do right now. See those people ahead of us? Watch how they enter the lift. Pay attention—do you see how it's done? Do you see how they sit down the moment the lift nudges against the back of their knees? That's what I need for you to do. Just put yourself into position when it's our turn, let the chair catch you before you sit down, and then either Jennifer or I will pull the bar over us so we don't fall out."

"Fall out?" she said. "We could fall out?"

"We're not going to fall out—that's what the bar is for. I'm just talking about the process."

"All of this is a non-issue," she said. "I've conquered mountains higher than this in my lifetime. Bring it on!"

"Oh, shit," Daniella said. "She's being way too cocky. I smell disaster..."

"I didn't hear that, Daniella!"

"Mom, I'm happy that you're doing this, but skiing is going to take some getting used to. I'm worried about you. Just go slowly, OK?"

"Slowly?" she said. "Look at how fast those chairs are fleeing those people away from us. This is no place to be slow. One must be on their game—and I can assure you, Daniella, that I *am* on my game."

When Blackwell said that, a striking man in his mid-fifties with dark hair graying at his temples turned around to look at Barbara. He was standing just in front of her, and when he looked at her, he lifted his goggles onto the top of his head, revealing eyes that were as blue as the sky. He was about Alex's height—tall and lean—with a dimple in his chin, and what clearly would have been a heavy beard if he didn't shave.

"Good morning," he said to Blackwell.

"Excuse me?" she said, surprised to hear a stranger speak to her, which rarely happened in Manhattan, but was the norm at a friendly ski resort in Maine.

"I said, 'good morning.' It sounds as if you're ready to ski."

"I'm sorry, but do I know you?"

He smiled when she said that, and when he did, it lit up a handsome face that was tan from perhaps too much time on the slopes. And yet for his age, which was damned close to Blackwell's, he was nevertheless well preserved, much like Barbara herself.

"You don't know me," he said. "But maybe we could meet?" He extended his hand to her. "I'm Marcus Koch," he said.

"You're Marcus *what*?"

"Koch," he said as she lifted her hat over her ears so that she could hear him better. "You know, as in 'Coke'."

"Oh!" she said. "Well, what a relief! I thought that you said—well, let's just say that it's best if it's left unsaid."

"Oh, my God," I heard Daniella whisper. "She thought that he said 'cock'."

"With this hat over my ears, I thought I heard something entirely different," Blackwell said. "How embarrassing. How deep into the basement of me. It's too early in the day to hear something like that." She shook her head as if to shake off the course the conversation was taking and then took his hand in hers. "Barbara Blackwell," she said. "Nice to meet you, Mr. Koch. Are you here to ski?"

"Am I here to what?"

"Oh," she said. "How silly of me. Of course you are. We are, after all, standing in line to board the lifts. And you are, after all, wearing a ski suit and skis. And other little ski bits...like your goggles and gloves, and that sort of thing."

Was this man rattling Blackwell? Could she, in fact, be attracted to him? I'd never blame her if she was—regardless of his age, he was hot. I couldn't imagine what he must have looked like in his youth. But since I'd never seen her interact with a man her age who appeared to be single and who was singularly good looking, I had to wonder whether she was indeed attracted to him. Because when did Blackwell ever stammer?

"Let me guess," he said. "You're new to this?"

"New, but nevertheless determined."

"You've never skied before?"

"Never. First time. Typically, I try to eschew the snow," she said as the line nudged forward.

"And yet look at you—completely prepared for the snow. I have to say that that's some suit you're wearing."

"You think? I wasn't sure. When I put it on, I was riddled with doubt even though it is Chanel."

"Where are you from?" he asked.

"Manhattan."

"Same here," he said. "But I have a home here, so when the season is ripe for it, I come to ski whenever I can."

"How outdoorsy of you."

"You could put it that way, I guess."

"You live in Manhattan?"

"Live and work."

"What do you do?"

"I'm a hedge fund manager."

Oh, shit, I thought. *This guy is totally loaded...*

"Which fund do you hedge?" Blackwell asked.

"Too long to go into that now," he said. "It looks as if I'm up next. Will you be at the lodge later tonight?"

"At the what?"

"There's a bar in the lodge," he said. "You know, in the building just behind you?"

"We only just arrived yesterday and this is my first time here. I haven't been to the lodge yet. Is the bar worth a go?"

"It is," he said as he slid away from her and claimed one of the lifts for himself. "So, you know, if I see you there tonight, I'd be happy to buy you a drink. Have fun, Barbara."

And then he was off.

"What in the fresh hell was that?" Daniella asked.

"A spark!" Alexa said.

"Hardly," Blackwell said.

"Oh, please," Daniella said. "You actually stumbled over your words—and when do you ever do that?"

"I only stumbled because I couldn't believe that a stranger actually spoke to me. And with what I initially thought was a vulgar-sounding last name."

"That's enough of that," I said. "We're up next. Let's go."

I took Cutter by the arm and lifted my lips to his ear. "She'll sit in the middle. You take one arm. I'll take the other. Does that work for you?"

"We've got this."

And surprisingly enough, when we positioned ourselves in front of the lift with Blackwell locked in our embrace, there were no issues. We all sat down, Cutter closed the bar over us, we held onto our poles—and off we went as

Daniella, Alexa, Brock, and Madison followed behind us in a separate lift.

"Well, that was an interesting exchange *you* just had," I said to Blackwell.

"Please. It was nothing short of a fleeting moment."

"Really? Because he straight out asked you if he'd see you at the lodge tonight. I'm pretty certain that he's hoping that your 'fleeting moment' together won't be that fleeting at all. I mean, come on—he was clearly coming on to you. All of us saw that. And he lives in Manhattan. And he's a hedge fund manager, for God's sake, which we all know means that he's practically printing money. And by the way, did you have a good look at him? He was beyond handsome."

"I see handsome men every day in New York—so what else is new? And I could care less about his money, assuming he has any."

"Hedge fund," I said.

"Fine. But what about his name? Koch! I thought for sure that he'd said something else. Something...subversive. But that was my mistake—and as embarrassing as it was, I'll own it. When he first introduced himself to me, I couldn't hear him with the lifts running and with my hat pulled over my ears. I'm sure that I looked like an idiot, but what am I to do about it now? Nothing. So? Onward."

"We are so going to the bar at the lodge tonight," I said. "He's going to be there. I know it."

"But to what end? Jennifer, I have zero interest in men at this point in my life—especially after what Charles did to me. I'm perfectly happy living my life with my friends and with my girls. I love my life as it is right now. Zero complications. I'm through with men, so can we just move beyond this? I mean, look around us," she said as we took the six-minute ride to the top of the mountain. "Even I have to admit that that the views are lovely. While I've certainly never been known as a snow bunny, I can tell both of you this—I might become one. At the risk of sounding like Alexa, just breathe in the fresh air right now—nothing like Manhattan. And take in the scent of the evergreens—nothing like Manhattan. And look at us—high above the tree line. It really is quite something—unlike this year's fall/winter collection, which was a goddamned disappointment."

"You are so deflecting."

"So what if I am? It's my choice to do so, and I won't hear another word of it. He simply engaged me. Am I supposed to react to a mere smile and a handshake? A flash of his bluer-than-blue eyes? Please. At this point in my life, I'm beyond that."

"But why not be open to it?"

"I've already told you why."

"All right," I said. "Fine. But I think you might be missing out on something here."

"On what? A chance greeting that took all of three minutes? I am not Daniella. I'm also not looking for someone to spend the rest of my life with. That part of my life is over with, and I'm fine with that. So, please—enough."

For now, I decided to let it go.

"Are you cold?" I asked her.

"I'm swaddled in my Chanel tampon, which is perfectly warm."

"Just checking!" I said.

As we rolled toward the top of the mountain, Blackwell apparently had a whole host of observations at the ready.

"Is that an eagle I see?" she asked about the bird flying toward us.

"That would be a crow," Cutter said.

"Well—how unAmerican of me."

A moment later: "Why are those people creating little snow globes down below us? How festive! How absolutely 'Christmas'. Should I learn to do that?"

"Let's just hope that you don't," I said. "Because all of those people you're seeing creating their little 'snow globes' are taking one digger after another. That's why the snow is exploding around them. They're tripping up and falling hard."

"Well, how perilous," Blackwell said. "If that's the case, those people are being reckless. And by the way, please don't tell me that you're taking *me* on *that* slope. Because now it looks completely inhospitable to me."

"Of course not. Cutter and I are taking you to the gentlest trail on the mountain. What I need for you to do is to just listen to Cutter and me when we depart the lift, and you'll be good."

"'Depart the lift,'" she said. "And how does one do that?"

"The lift doesn't exactly stop. It just pauses for a moment so we can get off when we reach our destination. When it does, we simply stand up, and then we ski away from it. After that, we're free to go wherever we like."

To my surprise, when we exited the lift, Blackwell dug in her poles and whisked herself away from it and us with unusual ease. Could she do nothing wrong? Might skiing for the first time actually be easy for her? She never ceased to amaze me. When Daniella, Alexa, Brock, and Madison departed their own lift and joined us, I turned around to welcome them, and when I did, I saw that Marcus Koch was just off to our right, speaking into his cell phone.

"Your cock is here, Mother," Daniella said. "And he's standing right over there."

"Can he even get reception up here," Alexa asked. "Or is he just stalling...?"

"Girls, get a grip," Blackwell said. "Why are you people making such a fuss over nothing?"

"Because of the way he looked at you?" Alexa said.

"Because of the way he flustered you?" Daniella said.

"Because he's beyond good looking," I said.

"Because of what Jennifer just said," Madison said.

"Enough!" Blackwell said. "Let's ski. What do I need to know before we tackle that slope? Cutter?"

"You're going to want to control your speed," he said. "That's first and foremost. To do that, all you need to do is turn your skis inward like this. See how I'm doing it? When you do that, the blades will cut into the snow, and you'll be in charge of how fast you go down the mountain. That is the number-one thing you need to know, so remember it."

"Got it," she said.

"Here's another tip," I said. "Ski from left to right, cut sharp and cut hard, because that also will slow your progress. What you don't want to find yourself in is a situation where you lose control and are suddenly going straight down the mountain at a breakneck pace. That could be disastrous. That said, if that does start to happen to you, just fall back on your ass before it becomes too late for you to regain control. When you're ready to go again, just pick yourself up, and start over. If you follow just those two simple instructions alone, I don't foresee any problems. I mean look around you—five-year-olds are up here. Since you haven't skied before, the slope will challenge you at first as you get your legs beneath you, but soon you'll get the hang of it."

"I'm about to crush it," she said. "Let's go!"

13

WHEN ALL OF us set off for the mountain's peak, it didn't escape my attention that Marcus Koch shot a sidelong glance at Blackwell as we pressed forward. And when we did, I heard him end his conversation, slip his phone back inside his suit, and start down the mountain at a leisurely pace.

Had he been waiting for us to begin? I wasn't sure, but it seemed that way. And what was I to make of that?

"Let's do this," Brock said.

"Amen," Madison said.

"Why do I suddenly feel paralyzed?" Blackwell said.

"Because shit just got totes to the real, Mom," Daniella said. "But you'll ace it. Just follow us. We'll be right beside you. And with us beside you, what can possibly go wrong?"

"Are you serious?" Blackwell said to her. "With all of you around me, everything could go wrong. I'm expecting a goddamned avalanche. Just let me start out on my own armed with the few tips Jennifer and Cutter have given me. If I start to spiral out of control, I'll just fall down on my back, as Jennifer suggested. Then I'll get up again and start over—because right now, I'm once again filled with resolve. This mountain isn't about to best me."

The moment she said that, she pushed away from us and started down the trail.

"Shit," I said. "Let's move it, everyone. I don't think she knows what she's in for."

"She doesn't," Alexa said. "She's always so overconfident. But maybe this will give her the lesson she needs when it comes to that."

"She could nail it," Brock said as he cut in front of me. "Who knows? I mean look at her—she's doing well."

And I had to admit that she was. She was skiing from left to right and she was keeping her speed in check by keeping the front of her skis pressed into one another, but the moment the mountain took its first dip, Blackwell didn't have the necessary skills to compensate for it, and she became unleashed.

With a shriek that was loud enough to catch the attention of all the skiers around us, Blackwell became an unhinged red flare shooting down the slopes.

"Turn in your skis!" Cutter shouted at her. "Cut left! Slow your momentum!"

"Fall!" I said as she picked up speed. "Just fall back and lay down!"

With an aggressive push, both Cutter and Brock broke away from the rest of us and hurried toward her.

"Help!" Blackwell cried out, her legs trembling beneath her as her pace quickened. "I'm going to die without seeing the spring/summer collection!"

With my poles, I dug in deep and gave myself a massive push so that I could pull in close behind Cutter and Brock. If she fell at this speed, she might injure herself. One of us needed to grab her by the arm and stop her short before that happened.

"What in the name of Chanel is happening to me!" she screeched.

And when those words rang out of her mouth, I saw Marcus Koch cut sharply to the left and stop abruptly so that he could turn to face her.

But it was too late for him.

Blackwell slammed straight into him with such force that they tumbled together down the slopes in a plume of powdery snow before finally slowing to a stop—with Blackwell firmly poised on top of the poor man.

Cutter, Brock, and I rushed to their side, with Madison, Daniella, and Alexa just behind us.

"Are you all right?" Koch asked her.

Their arms and legs were entangled. Both of them had lost their skis, goggles, and poles due to the accident. Their faces were so close to one another, and they were breathing so hard against each other that it was clear that the wrecking ball that was Blackwell had knocked the wind out of both of them.

"I'm so sorry," she said. "My God—how awful of me."

"Is it?" he asked with a disarming grin. "I mean, if two people were going to make a mess of it on a mountainside, at least we did it with style. Don't you think?"

Blackwell didn't respond to that. Instead, she said, "Did I hurt you?"

"I'm flat on my back with a beautiful woman on top of me. Believe me, I'm not feeling any pain."

"And how am I to respond to that?"

"Maybe with a smile?"

"Please. People are watching. Paparazzi might be taking our photographs. We must untangle ourselves."

"Paparazzi," he said. "Should I know you?"

"I'm a legend."

"Well, my mysterious legend, I think that getting out of this situation is going to be a bit of a challenge. Your right leg is hooked around my left knee in a weird kind of way. And I think that one of your bootstraps has somehow locked itself into one of mine. Are you able to remove it?"

"Well, of course I can. I'm fully capable of any task. Just maneuver your body to the left."

"I can't," he said. "You've got me pinned. And since you do, you know, maybe we should just stay like this for a while and get to know one another better."

"I hardly see that happening."

"You're a handful," he said. "Not that I mind that."

"You have no idea." She raised an eyebrow at him. "And by the way, that should terrify you."

"Sorry, but it doesn't."

"Then you should know that I eat cubes of ice for lunch," she said. "So—consider that."

"And yet you feel so warm against me. I wonder why that is..."

"If I feel warm against you, it's only because I just tumbled down a goddamned mountain."

"Hmmm," he said, looking her in the eyes. "I wonder if that's all it is..."

"Oh, bloody hell," she said looking up at us. "We can't stay like this forever. Cutter, Jennifer—somebody. Help us out!"

"You mean, before you get pregnant?" Daniella said.

Alexa actually giggled at her sister's comment, which came as a relief considering how those two had been going head-to-head with each other since we'd left New York.

"You did not just say that," Alexa said.

"I absolutely did. Look at them. I've experienced plenty of positions in my life, but I can tell you this with certainty, my dear little back-stabbing baby sister, that I've achieved nothing like what our mother and her apparent new suitor have managed to achieve—and for everybody to watch, I might add."

And at that, Daniella started a slow clap.

"Brava!" she said. "Well done, Mother. Way to class up those slopes."

"Daniella, please."

"He looks good on you, Mom. Or should I say that you look good on top of him?"

As Brock and Cutter tried to free them from each other, I heard Marcus ask Blackwell, "Who is that?"

"My ridiculous daughter."

"Your daughter? She must be in her early twenties. You look too young to have a daughter that age."

"Well," Blackwell said as Cutter tried to unlock their boots. "Thank you. How unusually kind of you. Even though I've likely just broken several limbs, I do try to take care of myself—as hard as that might be for you to believe right now."

"Look, Barbara," he said. "Since you nearly just took my life, you now officially must let me buy you a drink, if only to make amends. Meet me at the lodge tonight. Don't say no. It's just for one drink."

"Oh, look—the oldest line in the book! And what if I'm married? Have you considered that?"

"Are you?"

"Actually, I'm not."

"Divorced?"

"I hardly share my personal life with strangers."

"So, you're divorced. Been through one myself. I didn't like it when I caught my wife cheating on me."

Which is exactly what Charles had done to Blackwell. When Marcus said that to her, I saw something shift in her expression. For an instant, she seemed to assess him with new eyes.

"Just one drink—I promise," he said. "I'm here alone. My own children are with their mother, and it would be nice to spend some time with someone interesting for once."

"How do you know if I'm interesting? What if I'm dull and disappointing? What if I'm this kind of horror show off the slopes?"

"Yeah, I kind of doubt that."

"Well, at least you're intuitive," she said.

"I read people quickly."

"Is that so?"

"Actually, it is. I wouldn't have asked you for that drink if I thought it was going to be a waste of my time. Not in me."

"Shit is totes getting real," Daniella said beneath her breath.

"There," Brock said as he released whatever parts of their boots were hooked together. "You're free."

Then, in one swift, fluid motion, Marcus swept one foot beneath him, pressed down on it, and lifted Blackwell off of his body as he stood. He placed her gently in front of him with the sort of ease that suggested to me that this man was nothing if not muscular and fit.

"He's Iron Man," Alexa said.

"No shit," Daniella said. "Did you see that? I know Mom weighs next to nothing, but still. It was as if she was weightless. Good God."

"Are you all right?" Marcus asked her as Cutter brought

over their skis and Brock delivered their poles and goggles. "Nothing sprained or broken?"

"I'm as healthy as Chanel's bottom line."

"You do have a way with words," he said.

"You have no idea how I wield my words, Mr. Koch."

"Please, since you have, after all, been on top of me, at the very least call me by my first name. In case you've forgotten, it's Marcus."

"Fine, then—Marcus. Thank you for cushioning my fall."

"Is that what you call it?" He held up a hand before she spoke. "I'm joking," he said. "I'm just glad I was there to help stop you, because you really could have hurt yourself. It's still a long way to the bottom of the mountain, so be careful, OK?"

"After that scene, I'll walk down this damned mountain if I have to."

"And yet why do I feel as if you're about to put on those skis again, and give it another go? I don't know you, Barbara, but I can already tell that you're no quitter. So, see you at the bar in the lodge at eight?"

"I never agreed to that."

"You'll be there," he said as he lowered his goggles over his eyes. "I know you will. You have to come. We both know it."

"How utterly confident of you."

"That's the thing," he said. "I am confident, but not arrogant. I just want to share a drink with you—and after that blunder, you owe me that. So, I'll see you tonight."

"You must know that I am not to be had for the mere price of a mountain collision!" she said.

But when she said that, Marcus Koch had already swept away from us. Watching him ski down the slope, it was clear to me that he was an expert skier and had only chosen this slope in hopes of finding another opportunity to interact with Blackwell. He couldn't have known at the time how *that* was going to turn out, but their mountain mayhem was what it was—and being the romantic at heart that I was, I had to wonder if it had happened for a reason.

After we got down the mountain and back to the house, would Blackwell agree to going to the lodge's bar for a drink?

With her, one never knew.

14

"After tackling the same slope three times, Blackwell eventually became nothing short of the queen of the bunny slopes," I told Alex once we were alone in our bedroom, lying next to each other on our king-sized bed—exhausted after a day of skiing.

"I wish you could have seen it," I added as I snuggled next to him and put my head on his chest. We'd just returned to the house and peeled off our ski suits and now were wearing nothing but our underwear. I was in my bra and panties, and Alex was in nothing more than his boxer shorts. He wrapped his arm around my shoulders and held me close to him.

"After hearing that story, I kind of regret going off on my own," he said. "But I wanted to challenge myself. I wanted to take on that mountain in ways that would lift the stress of the past year from me. I took the most difficult trail I could find, I scored, and I feel more relaxed because of it. We really needed to get away, Jen."

"We did," I said. "And I'm glad that you had fun. You

needed to have that kind of release. This past year has been ridiculous."

"To say the least, but all of that's behind us now." He turned and kissed me on the lips, which my body immediately responded to. "I did miss you, though."

"I missed you, too. But now that Blackwell knows she can handle that slope on her own, you and I can ski together tomorrow—if there's time. Today, it was all about supporting Blackwell—even if we did fail to keep her from falling head-over-skis into that man's arms."

"And by the way, *that's* a story for the ages," Alex said. "I wish I could have been there to see it. Did either of the girls catch it on their SlimPhones?"

"No way—all of us were way too transfixed. It was like watching a car crash in slow motion. You wouldn't have believed it, Alex. It was as surreal as it was hilarious."

"Do you think she'll agree to go to the lodge tonight, knowing that he'll be there?"

"No idea. But if she resists, I plan on pressuring her into going. Because there's no question that sparks flew between them. When Blackwell was lying on top of him—utterly unable to extricate herself from him—he was flirting with her in ways that she tried to deflect, but he outsmarted her at every turn."

"I have a hard time imagining someone outsmarting her..."

"Well, imagine it. This Marcus guy was so on point, he totally took on Blackwell and won. As ridiculous as she was being, he just took it all in stride, and allowed her to be herself. She tried to throw him off his game, but every time she did so, he not only one-upped her, but it was clear to all of us that he was getting a kick out of doing so."

"It's going to take a special man to match Blackwell," Alex said.

"I think we might have found him."

"And I wonder how she feels about that? It's just been two years since she divorced Charles. And that divorce was ugly. Is two years enough for her to begin to trust another man again—if that's even what she wants? Because I'm not sure that she ever wants to be in a relationship again. She loved Charles. I think that what he did to her scarred her in ways that none of us will ever know." And then he shrugged. "But what do I know? I could be wrong—in fact, I hope that I am. Because I'd love to see Blackwell find a new man capable of maintaining a solid relationship. I don't want to see her go through the end of her life alone."

"Here's what I haven't told you. Since Blackwell had no choice but to talk to him when she was on top of him and attached to him, he brought up his own divorce. Apparently, he left his wife because she cheated on him. And when I heard him say that, I swear that I saw Blackwell's face soften, even if it was only for an instant, because that's what Charles did to her."

"In fact, it was the very reason she divorced his ass."

"Exactly. And Marcus divorced his wife for the same reason. Blackwell must be processing that now. Is he a man of principle? It certainly looks as if he is, and that alone could sway her to at least meet him for a drink."

"Look, anyone who knows Blackwell knows that if anything is going to come of this, she's going to wade into it very slowly. Her heart is so guarded right now that, if he does want to pursue her, it's going to take more than a few days to win her over. In fact, knowing her the way that I do, I'd say that it will take several months—if not a good year. Anyone who thinks otherwise is fooling themselves."

I swung my body around and straddled him. With my hands against his lightly hairy pecs, I looked down at him. "Enough of that for now. Where do you want to eat tonight? At the lodge? Or at one of the restaurants in town?"

"Why not check out the lodge? If we arrived at six, we could have dinner, and then maybe go to the bar, where Blackwell could meet up with Marcus. If she wants to."

"I plan on convincing her to."

"You know," he said as he gripped my ass. "Six o'clock is four hours away..."

"So, it is," I said, reaching behind me so I could grasp his cock, which was rock hard and throbbing beneath his underwear.

"Want to fool around, Mrs. Wenn?" he asked.

"Is that even a question, Mr. Wenn? Why don't you have your way with me? Right here, right now. Then, we can go into the shower, and you can take me there as well. That is, of course, if you have that kind of stamina left within you after your time on the slopes..."

The moment I said that, Alex lifted me straight off him, swept me around so that I was lying on my back, and slid down the length of my body. Then, he removed my panties, tossed them aside, and buried his face between my legs. His tongue probed so deeply within me, that I let out a moan of ecstasy and arched my back as his stubble brushed against my clit.

Wanting more, I extended my legs and hooked them around the back of his head, thus driving his mouth firmly against my sex, which I ground against him.

"You want to fuck me, don't you?" I said.

He looked up at me with a gleam in his eyes. "We're talking dirty now?"

"Looking at you right now? I want to get filthy."

"Careful what you wish for," he said.

"Says the man who hasn't even entered me yet..."

But when he did, Alex thrust into me so hard that my breath caught in my throat. I reached out and grasped the bedspread as he started to pound into me in ways that were just aggressive enough for me to enjoy. He swept my hair away from my face and leaned down to kiss me, and when he did, I could taste myself on his tongue. With his eyes never leaving mine, he removed my bra, dipped his head to one of my nipples, and bit down on it, sending a river of chills throughout my body—which I made every effort not to show to him. This was now a game between us—it was something we did often—and for me, it was so game on.

"Is that all you've got?" I asked.

"I think you know better."

"Then fuck me like you mean it."

"Like this?"

He pulsed even harder into me, but through it all—and as close as I came to coming on several occasions—I nevertheless challenged myself not to come while also taunting him.

"You really must be tired," I said as he whipped me onto my side, and came up behind me. Then, he lifted my right leg high into the air and entered me. "I can almost feel your fatigue."

"Is that so?"

I tried to keep a straight face when I said that, but it was nearly impossible. "In fact it is. Perhaps you need a nap."

And when I said that, both of us started to laugh.

"Oh, how I love you!" I said.

"You're a filthy minx," he said.

"I'm an alley cat!"

"You're a horny one, that's for sure."

"Finish me off, already!" I screamed.

"You're so going to get it now," he said. "Especially after that little performance of yours."

"Just keep knocking those jingle bells right against me, stud."

"You did not just say that…"

"Yes, I did. It's nearly Christmas. And this girl wants her presents to come early. So, bang me, Santa!"

And Alex did just that. For the next thirty minutes, we tossed ourselves around the bed in a whole host of positions —both old and new. There were points in our lovemaking when I wanted to ask, "And where did you learn *that* from?" But he was being so relentless with me—and I was too breathless to talk because of it. And when he finally brought me to climax, which was so earth-shatteringly loud, I hoped to God that no one in this mammoth mother of a house heard me.

Or him, for that matter. Because when Alex came?

He was just as loud as me.

15

LATER THAT NIGHT, for dinner, we decided to go to the Shipyard Brewhaus restaurant, which was located inside the lodge. It was a bit rustic for Blackwell's taste, but it actually turned out to be surprisingly good—the service was terrific, the drinks were on point, and in the end, everyone was happy.

But what came after dinner was questionable at best.

When all of us moved into the Widowmaker Lounge, which was packed with a mixed group of people, it quickly became clear to me and to all of the women in our group that we were completely overdressed.

As I looked around the space, I saw that most people were wearing jeans and casual sweaters—both men and women. Some of the older women had made an effort to step it up a notch, but only a few of them. So, if it didn't look as if we had hailed straight from the city before, it certainly did now.

"Why are there garish neon signs on the walls hawking something called 'Bud Light'?" Blackwell said. "And why do they call this place the 'Widowmaker Lounge,' of all things?

Are husbands about to die in front of me, leaving stricken widows in their wake? Where are we? Who am I? How did I get here? What in the hell kind of a bar is this?"

"Just relax," I said. "I'm sure they'll pour you a perfect martini. This might not be what you're used to in New York, but that doesn't mean that you can't let down your bob and have some fun for one night. So, buck up, Babs—because we *are* going to have some fun."

"Don't ever call me 'Babs' again."

"How about if I get the first round?" Cutter asked. "It would be my pleasure."

"Why are you so nice?" Daniella asked. "Why do you continue to drop your lure in front of me in ways that make me want to take a bite?"

This time, without flinching, Cutter just looked at her. "Let me see if I've got this right?" he said. "Martini? No olives, but with a twist?"

"You see? You even know my drink."

"It's not as if I don't pay attention to you, Daniella," he said to her with a smile. Then, he took everyone else's order, and turned away from us and went to the bar.

"And what am I to make of that?!" Daniella said.

"Zip," Blackwell said. "Trust me. He's off-limits."

"And trust *me* when I say that somebody has just spotted you," I said in a low voice to Blackwell.

"Oh, Christ. Hell has apparently come to roost in Christmastown. I'm assuming you mean Marcus? That *is* the reason all of you dragged me here. Where is he?"

"At the other end of the room, coming our way. And, oh my—does he ever look good. You couldn't really see his physique in his ski suit, but you can pretty much see all of him now. And holy shit. He's got to be a total fitness freak.

Look at that body of his. And how well he's dressed. You've got to give it to him, Barbara—that has to impress even you."

"Fine," she said as she looked over at him. "He is handsome. As for what he's wearing, I approve—especially for this joint. Prada jeans. A fitted, black Dior Homme cashmere turtleneck sweater. And black boots—also by Prada. And then there's his watch, which I have to say is the real standout. I recognize it immediately. Impressive."

"You can see his watch from here?"

"I can see everything from here."

"What is it?"

"A Jaeger-LeCoultre Master Control Grand Tourbillon surrounded by sapphires and twenty carats of beveled diamonds, which might sound feminine—but not when you see it in person. It's absolutely masculine. And just so you know, it costs five hundred grand. The fund he hedges must be successful."

"Well, that should perk up your nips," Daniella said. "Or moisten your panties. Either way, if you don't want him, I'll totally take him. He's totes working that hot daddy look. Just look at that strong jawline of his, not to mention his thick head of dark hair, which is just starting to gray at the temples. If you don't want to get into the sack with that piece of man meat, Mom, I sure as hell will."

"Like hell you will—he's practically your father's age."

"Your point? That just means that he's likely been through enough women to have mad skills in the bedroom. Think about that for a moment, Mommie Dearest—and what it could mean for you..."

"Quiet—he's almost upon us."

"Hello," Marcus said as he approached us. He was holding in his left hand what looked like a glass of Scotch on the rocks, and he looked directly at Blackwell when he said, "I'm glad that you decided to come."

"Well," she said. "It's not as if I had a choice. I was practically abducted."

"No other reason?"

"I'm sorry?"

"Doesn't matter. You look beautiful, Barbara. You've brought Manhattan to Maine."

"It needed to be done," she said. "Just look around us —so many sordid tales of Wal-Mart woe. Though I do have to admit that you're also lifting the room, Mr. Koch—"

"Marcus," he said.

"All right," she said. "Marcus. I'm fairly certain that a space like this doesn't see a watch like that very often. Did you wear it for show?"

"I wear this watch every day. I don't do anything for show," he said.

When he said that, Cutter turned and started to hand us our drinks. It was pretty much martinis in various forms for all of us. The only exception was the tall glass of Guinness Cutter had ordered himself, but only because Alex had told him on the drive over that he was off duty tonight—and that he fully expected Cutter to join in the festivities. Otherwise, Alex and I both knew that Cutter would have chosen something non-alcoholic. We wanted him to be a part of the evening, not removed from it. It wasn't as if something was going to happen to us here.

"I have a table just over there, if you'd like to join me," Marcus said to Blackwell. "I'd be honored if you would."

"But I'm here with my friends," she said in a last-ditch effort to deflect. "And with my daughters. Leaving them would be rude, don't you think?"

"As one of her daughters, I have zero problem with that," Alexa said.

"And as her more stylish daughter, neither do I," Daniella said. She extended her hand to him, which he shook. "It's nice to meet you again, Marcus," she said. "I'm Daniella. The other one is my poor sodden sister, Alexa. So, please—sweep Mother away from us so the rest of us can play. Believe me, you'll be doing all of us a favor."

"OK," he said, shrugging at Blackwell. "So, what do you say?"

"She'd love to join you," Alex said as he pressed his hand against Blackwell's back and urged her toward him. "We'll just be here at the bar. Whenever both of you would like to join us again, please do. I'm Alex, by the way. And this is my wife, Jennifer, whom I believe you've already met, along with my cousin Brock, his girlfriend Madison, and our good friend Cutter."

"It's nice to see all of you again," Marcus said. "Especially under less dire circumstances. Though I am happy those circumstances happened, especially since nobody got hurt."

"Speak for yourself," Blackwell said. "My pride was hurt."

"And yet somehow, you rose above it to become one of the room's stars."

"One of the room's stars? You mean that there are others here? Have you even looked around?"

"I have. The others would be your daughters, Jennifer, and Madison."

"Well, how quick of you," she said.

"You'd be surprised by how quick I am."

"Then I guess you'll have to surprise me."

Did Blackwell just flirt with him...?

Whatever it was, I needed to urge her on. "So, we'll see you both whenever," I said as Blackwell approached him. "We'll be here all night, so take your time."

And with that, I saw Blackwell's shoulders stiffen a little as she followed Marcus into the crowd and toward the table he had reserved for them.

"I'm transfixed!" Daniella said.

"He seems like a nice man," Alexa said. "He might be rich as hell, but you wouldn't know it—he didn't come off as arrogant, and I sensed zero pretension in him. And the way he breezed through Mother's ridiculous banter proves that he has a sense of humor and that he's a gentleman. It's time for Mom to give someone else a chance—especially after what Dad did to her. She thinks she's too old to find love again, which is ridiculous. What do you think, Daniella?"

"That you're a full-on lesbian in sheep's clothing."

Alexa sighed. "Beyond that?"

"I'm just joking, Alexa. And of course, I agree. And I'm encouraged. So, let's see how this turns out. Because I'm with you. I also think that Mom deserves a second chance. Even if this comes to nothing, it's something, right? She has put up a good front since she and Dad divorced, but through it all, having someone as hot and as successful as Marcus come after her can't exactly hurt her self-esteem. I think that everyone sees our mother as somebody who's above it all and invincible, which is exactly how she wants to be seen. But there are other layers beyond the mask that only those close to her can sense. Maybe that Marcus guy can get her back into the game again. And hell," Daniella said. "Maybe he'll even be the one—who knows? Time will tell, I guess. Now—let's all get into position so that we can spy on them! Because there's no way in hell that I'm going to miss this shit."

16

"YOU ARE GOING to miss this shit," Alex said. "Your mother feels self-conscious enough as it is. She doesn't need us hovering over her just so we can watch whatever transpires between them. Would you want that kind of scrutiny?"

"No," Daniella said. "But you have to know that it's going to kill me not to watch. I want to see if they really do have a connection. Because I want that for Mom. I want her to find love again."

"And I get that," Alex said. "I know that's important to you and to Alexa. After they spend some time together and join us again, I think we'll all have a fairly good idea whether or not a connection was made. So, why don't we all step over here—at the corner of the bar? It's less-crowded there."

"And there are boys over there," Daniella said as we moved to the end of the bar. "Lot's of them. I was so focused on Mom and Marcus, I didn't realize just how many presumably single men are here tonight. And a lot of them are hot."

"I thought that you were off men," I said.

"For like five minutes, I was. But looking around right

now? I'm all in again." She glanced over at Cutter. "Unless Cutter wants to do something about that," she said.

"Leave Cutter alone," I said. "In fact, if you were focused and paying attention, I believe you would have noticed that there's a young man right over there who's checking you out right now."

"What man? Over where?"

"Are you able to be discreet? Because I'm not sure that's even possible for you."

"Of course I can be discreet."

"I guess we'll see, so at least try to be." I gave a slight nod directly in front of me while I sipped my martini. "Do you see the group of five guys at that table over there?"

Daniella raked her hair away from her face, turned so she could glance around the room, and then turned back to me.

"I see them," she said.

"Actually, that *was* discreet. Well done. Did you see the dark-haired young man in the navy-blue sweater? Because he's the one who I caught checking you out."

"I didn't get that close of a look."

"Then give it a minute, and look again."

Once she had, she turned back to me, and said, "He's totally hot!"

"Are we talking about the same guy?" Alexa said. "The one with the dimples? Yes? I thought so. Because I actually think that he's checking *me* out. In fact, I'm sure of it."

"No one is looking at you, Alexa," Daniella said. "Sure, you've whipped yourself into shape for another night and I've already admitted that you look good in your ridiculously expensive sleeveless Mugler top. But here's what you don't have that the boys want—sexual experience, which I totes have with an exclamation point."

"Because you're a slut."

"Because I'm no prude. And that boy over there? He can smell my experience like a rose held to his nose. Sorry, but I win this one. He's looking at me."

"I don't think so," Alexa said. "And I'm not being catty. Your back is to him—mine isn't. He keeps smiling at me. And now he's just lifted his beer to me."

"The hell he did."

"Actually, he did," I said. "I saw it."

"How can this even be?" Daniella said.

"There are plenty of other men here, Daniella," Alex said. "So what if he likes Alexa? Look around. You're a beautiful girl. I get that you want to flirt. So find someone else to flirt with."

"Don't you get it?" she said. "I can't lose him to her. That would be the end of me. It would be an injustice!"

"Then that's what's coming your way," Brock said. "Because he is coming this way—and he's looking straight at Alexa."

"Daniella, you're going to lose this one," Cutter said. "So why don't you come over here and enjoy your drink with me?"

"Excuse me?" she said.

"Come and enjoy your drink with me."

"Why are you suddenly sounding all alpha right now?"

"Maybe because that's what you need. As wild and as reckless as you come off, I'm beginning to think that most of it is an act. The more that I come to know you—especially from our time on the island, where you showed everyone the person you really are at heart, and when you never left my side when things became dire for me —the more I get the feeling that you act up because you've been hurt too many times, and because you haven't been treated properly by a real man. So, maybe you're due for one."

"What are you saying? Are you talking about *you*?"

He shrugged and sipped his beer. "I don't know—who knows? But how about if you drop the façade and show me who you really are? I've seen that person a few times, but not often enough. So, why don't you remind me who she is —and maybe even remind yourself in the process?"

"Now I'm feeling weirdly claustrophobic," she said. "As if everyone is just holding their breath, wondering what's going to fly out of my mouth."

When no one responded to her, Daniella looked absolutely stripped bare and vulnerable. Her features softened, and then she bit her lower lip and clearly became tense.

"You know how I feel about you, Cutter. I've certainly laid *that* bare to the world in ways that will forever haunt me. If you're just trying to be nice—don't. I've been disappointed enough this year. I don't think that I could take another hit—especially if it came from you."

"I don't plan on delivering one," he said. "I'd just finally like to get to know the real Daniella. So, why don't we make that happen? A table just opened up right over there. Let's go sit down and talk."

He put his hand on her shoulder, causing Daniella's cheeks to flush in ways that made her look downright terrified to me. And I knew why—she was in love with Cutter. She always had been. The way he was reaching out to her now was likely surprising and overwhelming her on a whole host of levels—fear of putting her heart on the line for the man she truly loved and terror at the thought of having it crushed if nothing came of whatever was happening between them now.

I didn't know why Cutter was doing this, but I did know

him well enough to know that he wasn't insensitive and that he certainly was no fool—when it came to Daniella, he knew for a fact that he was dealing with a sensitive situation. And I knew that he'd never intentionally hurt her.

So, I had to wonder if he was indeed interested in her. Did he see another side of her that was worth getting to know? At first, I wondered how anyone could—on the surface, that girl was nothing short of a terror. But he had just evoked within me a memory, and that was of our time on the island, when Daniella had stayed at Cutter's side from the moment he was brought back to us, just a whisper away from death. For hours on end, she'd sat next to him and held his hand, she'd assisted in cleaning his wound, she'd gone looking with her sister for natural antibiotics for him, and I'd witnessed myself her praying for him and trying to communicate with him even as he became more delirious as time wore on.

Clearly, there was a part of Cutter that remembered her commitment to him and all that she'd done for him during that time. Maybe that's why he'd asked her to drop her façade and to show him the real Daniella again.

As they walked away from us, I took Alex's hand.

"Can you believe this?" I asked.

"Not at all."

"What in the hell is going on?"

"No clue."

"Cutter knows that he can't cross that kind of line with her without good reason. He's a good man—he just wouldn't do that. He must feel that there might be something there. You remember how she cared for him on the island. When we got him back, she always was there for him. Is that the root of this?"

"I don't know. Because what I also remember is how she

threw herself at his feet and pleaded for him to marry her in our apartment."

"But she does love him," I said. "You have to admit that."

"I think it's clear to all of us that she does love him. The question is whether she can grow up, rein it in, and be worthy of him. Because Cutter is a good man. He's a catch."

"How old is he again? Twenty-seven?"

"Twenty-seven."

"And Daniella just turned twenty-three. A four-year age gap isn't that big of a deal, as you and I know. We're nearly four years apart in age. And she's a stunning girl—I'm sure that, despite her theatrics, on some level Cutter must find her physically attractive."

"There's no question about that. Daniella's a knock-out."

"Who in the hell saw this coming?" I said as I sipped my martini.

Alex touched his glass against mine. "Or what will come of it?"

I nodded over at Alexa. "Look at Alexa. She now has three young men talking to her. And all of them are perfectly cute. She needs something like this, if only because Daniella always is the one who seems to get the attention."

"Alexa is certainly getting her share of it now. She's probably lecturing them on world peace. Or the importance of free-range chickens. Global warming. You know—the gambit. But at least they seem interested. I mean, look at them, for God's sake. All eyes on her."

"And good for her. But just wait until Blackwell hears about all of this."

"Yeah, about that one," he said. "I wonder how that's going?"

"Well, she hasn't come back yet. So, that's telling.

Because God only knows that woman suffers no fools, and she would have been back here in a hot second if she thought that she was dealing with one."

"True dat."

"Really?" I said.

He winked at me, and then leaned over and kissed me. "Just keeping it fresh."

"You've been especially fresh lately, especially in the bedroom."

"Just trying to keep the wife happy."

"And you're succeeding like a type-A overachieving all-star."

I looked over at Brock and Madison, who at this point only had eyes for each other. Brock was leaning with his back against the bar, Madison had her back pressed against his chest, and they were clearly flirting with each other.

"Look at those two," I said. "Unaware of anything but themselves."

"As it should be."

I turned to Alex. "We've built one hell of a family, you know?"

"In fact, I do know. What we have now is something neither of us had when we were growing up. We deserve this. Both of us were cheated of it for most of our lives. And yet now we finally have a real family. Friends who are far more than mere friends. And I'm grateful for it."

"Do you even know how much I love you?" I said.

"I think I do, but I never tire of hearing it, Mrs. Wenn."

"With all of my heart," I said as I kissed him on the lips. "You are my Christmas miracle. The best thing that has ever happened to me. How did a girl like me ever get so lucky to find a man like you?"

"I could ask a similar question," Alex said. "Because you,

Jennifer, are not only the love of my life, but you've changed my life in ways that you'll never know or even fathom. But at the very least, I hope that you feel at your core what you do mean to me. Because it's beyond substantial. To me, it's the world. I love you, Jennifer. Deeper than I think you'll ever know."

IT WAS NEARLY CLOSING time when Blackwell and Marcus rejoined the group. Daniella and Cutter were off somewhere chatting, which had to be a good sign since they'd been gone for two solid hours now. As for Alexa, she now was with Alex, Brock, Madison, and me—and she was glowing.

"What's happened to you?" Blackwell said to Alexa as she approached us with Marcus at her side. "You look as if you've been turned into a furnace."

"I've just had a wonderful night, that's all," she said.

"And why is that?"

"I'll tell you later."

"Well, whatever it is, I'm glad to hear it. I want you to be happy, my dear. Sometimes, I worry that you aren't."

"Tonight, I was."

"Then perfect." She hesitated for a moment before she said, "And I have to say that so was I. Marcus has been an excellent companion. I think we'd still be talking now if these horrid people weren't about to close the doors on us."

Marcus laughed when she said that, and then he concurred. "In fact, I know we would," he said.

Oh, my God! They did make a connection! And he totally gets her sense of humor!

"Where is Daniella?" Blackwell asked. "And Cutter? This place has already taken to the bullhorns and given last call, so we should probably leave before they toss us out into the snow."

"They actually took to one of the tables and have been hanging out together for a couple of hours," I said as casually as I could. "Alexa, would you mind telling them that we're about to go?"

"Not at all."

When she walked away from us, Blackwell skewered me with her eyes. "Since when do those two 'hang out' for a couple of hours?"

"We'll talk more about it later, OK? As in tomorrow morning. Not now."

"You're nothing short of a shrill of secrets," she said.

"I am not. Right now isn't the best time...because here they come. Hi, you two!" I said as Daniella and Cutter approached us with Alexa.

"What in the fresh hell is this?" Blackwell said beneath her breath to me.

If only so as not to embarrass them, I ignored her.

"They've given last call, so we should leave," I said.

"Maine," Daniella said. "If we were in Manhattan, we'd still have hours ahead of us. But I've had a great time," she said. "Thanks for bringing all of us here, Alex and Jennifer. I appreciate it."

"You're perfectly welcome, Daniella," Alex said.

"One thing," Blackwell said. "Marcus is here on vacation alone. I hope that I haven't stepped on anyone's toes, but I've invited him to our little cocktail party tomorrow night for Christmas Eve. Is that OK?"

And when she said that, I felt my heart jump.

"Of course it is," I said as calmly as I could. "We'd love to have you join us, Marcus. But just to warn you, it's going to be a dressy affair. We're also not going to have a formal dinner—that will happen on Christmas Day, which you certainly are invited to, as well. As for tomorrow night, we're just going to gorge ourselves on a whole host of hors d'oeuvres, which will take the place of dinner itself."

"Well, thank you," he said. "And here I thought that I was going to spend Christmas Eve alone. This trip is turning out to be the bright spot of my year."

"We look forward to seeing you tomorrow night. Eightish?"

"Works for me. Barbara already has given me the address."

Has she? Well, then...

"Perfect," I said. "Then we'll see you tomorrow!"

17

EARLY THE FOLLOWING MORNING, while Alex continued to snore lightly in our bed, I got out of bed, put on my white satin robe, and went to Blackwell's bedroom. She reared straight up in the bed when I woke her, and then I asked her to follow me to the kitchen.

It was just five o'clock and we'd only gotten a few hours of sleep, but I knew that she wanted questions answered about Daniella and Cutter, and it was best to answer them while we were alone and everyone else was still asleep.

"Put the coffee on," she said as she tied her black robe around herself and we stepped into the kitchen. "I need several injections of it."

"You're not alone—I'm putting it on now."

"Why do I feel as if I'm hung over?"

"How many martinis did you have last night?"

"Marcus just kept ordering them. I have no idea—but likely way too many."

"So, you two got along?"

"If I say anything positive about my interactions with him, you're just going to start to map out the wedding."

"I will not. What was he like?"

"Before we get to that, why is your hair a horror show right now?"

"Seriously? I just got up."

"And you couldn't have even run a brush through it for me? I certainly did for you. Why is your husband still in love with you if you insist on getting up looking like rats have nested in your weave?"

"I don't have a weave. And my husband loves me just as much as I love him—with no bounds."

"Tell that to your divorce lawyer in two years."

"Oh, whatever. Why don't you tell me about Marcus before people start to wake up. We only have a limited amount of time to talk in private before that happens. So, come on—spill it!"

"I need coffee first."

"It's coming."

"Then we'll talk when it comes."

When the pot was filled, I poured her a cup—black, just as she liked it.

"And let's just thank God for this," she said as she took her first sip. "While there's a chance that I might still be slightly drunk, at least I can be awake through it all."

I poured myself a cup, added a bit of cream and Stevia to it, and then sat next to her at the island. "Tell me about him," I said.

"He's intriguing. He's handsome. He's worthy of a second glance."

"What did you two talk about? You were gone for hours."

"I don't know. We talked about everything. It seemed unusually easy talking to him. Maybe that was because he took the time to listen to me in ways that Charles never did. We talked about our children, about our divorces, about our jobs, and all sorts of meaningless trivia along the way."

"Did you have fun?"

"Define 'fun'."

"Why are you always so difficult?"

"Define 'difficult'."

"Jesus! Did you enjoy yourself, or not?"

She blew over her cup of coffee and then just rolled her eyes at me. "Well of course I did. I didn't invite him to Christmas Eve because I loathed him. As I said, he's intriguing. I enjoyed how easy it was to talk with him. He's bright. He's intuitive and disarmingly funny. And I liked how his mind worked—we talked a lot about business. He's savvy—and clearly successful. I find that attractive. But we only talked for a few hours, so don't get your panties in a knot over any of this, because I'm certainly not. When you turn my age, Jennifer, and have been through a failed marriage—which I hope will never happen to you—you become very guarded. It's a cliché, but your heart truly does become a steel trap. And it's wounded and bruised. That said, I did enjoy myself. He seems like a perfectly nice man, so we'll see what tonight brings—and if he remains equally disarming. But enough about him. What I want to know is what Cutter and Daniella were up to."

Since I knew that was weighing heavily on her mind, I just got to it and told her everything I knew.

"*Cutter* started this?" she said.

"He did."

"But why? I love my daughter deeply, but everyone knows that she's a goddamned train wreck. Where did this come from? Cutter isn't stupid—he sees what all of us see in her. A monsoon! He's so on the straight and narrow when it comes to his life. I'm sorry to say that I just can't see him inviting Daniella into it, as much as it pains me to say that. I want Daniella to find love, but with Cutter? I can't see that happening—and that's strictly between us."

"Everything being said right now is between us."

She took a sip of her coffee. "You know, I love that boy—and if my daughter could finally get her shit together, I'd love nothing more than for her to be with him. But I'm confounded that we're even discussing this. What is all this about? Please enlighten me. Because I don't understand any of it."

"Here's what Alex and I discerned. When Cutter was talking to Daniella before they went off to a table of their own, he mentioned the time that Daniella had spent with him when his life was on the line on the island. You remember how she was there for him when we thought we were going to lose him—she was at his side in ways that none of us were. I think he's thought long and hard about that over these past few months, and perhaps questioned who Daniella really is as a person because of that. She's a complicated girl."

"The understatement of the decade."

"But she also can be a wonderful person—we all know that because we've witnessed it for ourselves. I think that Cutter saw the real Daniella when she was there for him. That girl did everything she could to make sure that he left that island alive. And don't forget that when Cutter was first returned to us, he was still coherent. I think it was at that point that he remembers what Daniella did for him. After that, he became too sick to remember any of it. And I believe that with the passing of time—and with some serious reflection—that has come to mean something to him. He knows Daniella's potential. Last night, he said to her that he thought she acted up because she had been hurt by too many men, and that maybe what she really needed was a real man to bring out the person he remembered on that island."

"Well, I would agree with that. Daniella tends to hook up with losers—not to sound like Donald Trump, but it's true. She has a serious case of low self-esteem that reveals itself in the worst of ways."

And then Blackwell paused for a moment. "You know, the divorce was especially hard on Daniella," she said. "Because Daniella was nothing if not a Daddy's girl. Before Charles and I separated, she never acted like this. But the moment the papers were signed and the divorce was settled, she became this completely different person. She went to hell. So, all of her behavior is likely on me because I'm the one who initiated that divorce."

"What were you to do? Charles cheated on you. Were you supposed to stay in that marriage given what he'd done to you?"

"Many others would have," she said. "For their families. I chose not to for two reasons. First, when I learned about what he'd done to me and to our family, he was dead to me. Second, I wanted to set an example for my daughters, so they'd know that no man ever should treat them like that— and if one did, they needed to dump his ass and move forward with their lives, just as I have. While that sounded right to me at the time, I'm fairly certain that my decision might have affected Daniella more than it did Alexa, who is more rational than her sister. And that kills me."

"How could you have stayed with him after what he'd done to you?" I asked. "You couldn't. However Daniella and Alexa have interpreted the situation, what you showed them are character and strength. Hopefully, what Daniella will eventually take away from your decision to leave Charles is that no woman in a committed relationship should ever remain with a partner who cheats on her. By divorcing Charles, you sent a solid, meaningful message to your girls. You said that you were better than that, and by doing that alone, you essentially told Daniella and Alexa that they also should never tolerate that kind of behavior in their own relationships."

"I think that Alexa gets it, but not Daniella," she said. "Alexa hasn't changed the way that Daniella has, but then Daniella always was closer to her father than Alexa was—and she's always been the more emotional one. Psychologically, I think that she was the one who was most damaged by our divorce. And that damage has revealed itself in ways that many of us would rather forget. She hasn't been herself since I filed papers. She's not the sweet girl I remember from before the divorce. She's regressed to the point that she's become intolerable. I think that she's seriously been affected by the divorce. I mean, look at her now—a combative mess. I'm directly responsible for that. Charles fought to save our marriage, but I was having none of it. The girls know that I walked away from our marriage, for better or worse."

I placed my hand on her arm.

"I do adore you, you know?" she said.

"Well you are, after all, my surrogate womb."

"Please, for the love of God, stop saying that."

I gave her a kiss on the cheek and told her that I loved her.

"I love you, too," she said. "Somehow, as unfathomable as it is to me, you've managed to become my third daughter."

"Who knew?" I said.

"Who knew, indeed?"

"Well, I guess that all we can do now is let the day play

out and see how tonight goes," I said. "After last night with Cutter, Daniella has a lot on her mind right now, and she's probably had a fitful sleep. She knows that if she doesn't straighten up, her chances with Cutter are in serious question. As for Cutter, I'm sure he's processing his own feelings for her and what transpired between them last night. He might even be awake right now, wondering to himself how to move forward—if he even wants to move forward."

"Let's just pray that he does," Blackwell said. "Because he's the one who decided to open that door, and I know my daughter. If she does rein herself in and he nevertheless decides to take a step back? God help us all. And God help him if he does so, because he's the one who started this— and if he ends it with no good reason, then I'll end it with him in ways that boy won't soon forget."

18

THE REST of the day went off without a hitch—and thank God for that.

Cutter and Daniella went off for a walk in the early afternoon, and that walk was a constant source of speculation for Alexa, who was dumbfounded by the lot of it—not that anyone could blame her. Still, since none of us wanted any drama between those two, we refused to engage her.

It was Christmas Eve and with the caterers set to arrive at six to prepare the many hors d'oeuvres that would take the place of a formal dinner, there were things to get done, especially since we had a guest arriving at eight—Marcus Koch. So, despite Alexa's repeated questions about Daniella and Cutter, we set about making the house look as festive as possible.

I tended to the music, because I loved Christmas music. It was hellish growing up with my abusive, alcoholic parents, whom I still had no contact with to this day. But it was Christmas music that I leaned on during the holidays of my early years to partly allow me to escape from reality. The music allowed me to lose myself in the spirit of the season in ways that my parents' behavior denied me.

As a child, I would take to my bedroom and listen mostly to Barbara Streisand's iconic first Christmas album, if only because it evoked the kind of sadness that I could relate to at that point in my life.

Christmas was never a happy time for me as a child, and because of that, her album spoke profoundly to me. I remember when my mother asked me why I kept "playing those songs over and over again." I never answered her truthfully, because if I did and she learned just how miserable she and my father made me, I feared I'd receive a beating, so I just told her that I loved Streisand's voice—which even my mother had to admit she enjoyed.

But it wasn't all dour for me when I was a kid. Growing up, I also listened to Mariah Carey's first Christmas CD, "Merry Christmas," which I still considered among the best Christmas albums ever. And then there was Ella Fitzgerald's "Ella Wishes You a Swinging Christmas," Bing Crosby's 1945 album "Merry Christmas," and 1973's "A Motown Christmas," and a whole host of others that seemed to speak directly to me—as if they were reaching out to me, and understanding me in ways that so few did.

Even after all these years, I still loved those albums. They weren't only classics, but amazing works of art that had brought me a great deal of happiness during my darker, younger years. And now? Now they lifted me up in this amazing new phase of my life, which was all about love— being loved by Alex and all of my friends, and the love that I had for them.

As I chose the playlist for later that night, I reached deep into my past in an effort that I hoped would touch all of us. I chose each song carefully, and after I'd set up a proper playlist on my SlimPhone, which I'd later connect to the house's Bose sound system, I was pleased with my choices. A mix of upbeat, popular Christmas songs interlaced with songs that made you want to pull your family in close to you and tell them that you loved them.

Because that's what this season is all about...

Meanwhile, everyone around me was busy. Madison and Brock were in the kitchen making certain that every wine glass, martini glass, and tumbler sparkled. They also were unloading boxes of champagne and different kinds of white wine into the refrigerator. Bottles of vodka and gin were already stacked in the freezer.

Blackwell and Alexa were tending to the flowers that had been delivered earlier via the only florist in the area, and they were placing them strategically around the house in a number of vases—tall and short. And because of the few inches of late-morning snow we'd received earlier, Alex was outside shoveling the walk to make certain that when Marcus arrived, he wouldn't slip and fall.

After the year all of us had gone through, there was something in the air that galvanized how special tonight needed to be for all of us, if only because there was a clear sense that we wanted the year to end on a positive note.

This year had been rotten in so many ways, but it hadn't defeated us—it hadn't brought us down—and because it hadn't, we needed to rejoice in that. We were here together, we were alive together, we were stronger because of what we'd endured, and we were thriving and happy because of it.

For me, it was tonight that meant the most to me—not Christmas morning, with its wealth of gifts. As appreciative as I was to receive any gift that someone had put time, thought, and effort into purchasing for me, what I loved most about the season was spending time with those whom I loved.

That's what mattered to me.

Tonight, we would dress up, we would mix, we would laugh, and we would salute ourselves for getting through one of the toughest years of our lives. No present could ever be more meaningful than that, nor could it trump spending time with my family and my extended family— telling them that I loved them, joking with them and hell, just being with them. Especially with my husband. My darling Alex.

After this year—and especially after the loss of our child —I was beyond grateful that I was here, that Alex and I were closer than we'd ever been, and that all of us could come together to celebrate not only our lives together, but the fact that we'd won in a year that for so long seemed determined to destroy us.

IT WAS mid-afternoon when my SlimPhone rang, and when I pulled it out of my pants pocket, my heart soared—Lisa!

"I'm so happy that you called!" I said.

"And I'm beyond grateful that you even dared to answer!"

"What does that mean?"

"You think that Maine is remote? Forget it. Maine might as well be Manhattan considering where I am right now. As you know, I'm in Tank's hometown of Prairie Home, Nebraska. But what you don't know is the massive size of its population—2: *his parents*."

"Oh, dear," I said.

"You don't even know."

"But where are you now?" I asked. "If you're in a place that's so rural, how can your cell reception be so good?"

"Tank and I might have needed a little time away. We might have taken a day trip to Lincoln, where there are actual signs of life."

"Oh, burn!" I said. "So, you did it! You totally are at a no-tell motel!"

"And so what if we are? As if you weren't in one yourself this time last year. I've merely learned from the best."

"Well, one does have to do what one has to do..."

"And so we have—if only to have sex. Because my fears about his parents' house sadly proved true! It's so small that Tank and I both know they would be able to hear us if we even tried to make love. So, that's not happening. That said, I'm now alone in my sordid little no-tell motel and can talk freely. Tank just left for one of the local supermarkets to get me a bottle of the Goose, a lemon, and vermouth, and himself a six-pack of Guinness. And do you want to know why? Because his parents don't drink!"

"Who the hell doesn't drink?"

"His parents! It's been hell. You have no idea. God, I wish we were with you all."

"I also wish that you were here—more than you know. But if you two are going to marry soon, you know that you needed to do this. You had to meet his parents. So, tell me— how do you like them?"

"Look, they are perfectly nice people. In fact, they are probably too fucking nice. I swear to God that when his mother learned that I wrote about zombies, she totally genuflected right in front of me and shot Tank's father an utter look of horror and concern, likely for her son's well being."

"Tank hadn't shared with them what you write about?"

"Apparently, he hadn't. Maybe he knew better. But the zombies are out of the bag at this point, and let's just say that they are happily eating their way through my holiday."

"When do you leave?"

"Same day as you—the day after Christmas."

"Well, here's the good news—you just need to get through today and tomorrow, and then you'll both be on a plane and back in Manhattan the next day."

"Where I'll need to see a shrink. How is everything going there?"

"Oh, honey, you wouldn't even believe it if I told you."

"What does that mean? Give me the deets. I'm hungry for deets! And drama! And a laugh! After spending time in Prairie Home, NObraska, where nothing at all happens, I'm dying for some drama to come into my life right now. So, spill it! What am I missing—because I need to live again!"

"Blackwell met a suitor."

"Oh, no, she didn't. Not without me there to see it, she didn't."

"I'm telling you that she did."

"She met a man?"

"Yes!"

"Tell me everything."

I told her everything.

"And he's coming to spend Christmas Eve with you tonight?"

"He is!"

"Well, sweet baby Jesus," Lisa said. "Blackwell never would have invited him if she didn't feel that there was some sort of spark between them."

"Oh, there was a spark. First on the slopes, and then later at the bar."

"I'm missing everything!"

"You don't even know. Because you want to know what else you don't know?"

"And cry into my pillow because I'm missing it? Fine —torture me."

"Girl, you need to sit down for this one."

"I am sitting down."

"Then you need to lie flat on your back and get ready to take this one in the gut."

"Punch me!" she said.

"Something is happening between Daniella and Cutter."

"Bullshit," she said.

"It's true."

"What does that even mean? Daniella is a mess. Cutter knows that, and he'd never tolerate her even at her best— whatever that is. How can this even be?"

I told her everything I knew, and about what I thought had brought them together at this point.

"Well, when you put it like that, I have to say that it's true," she said. "More than any of us, Daniella was the one who was by his side the most when those motherfuckers returned him to us. And you're right—he wasn't completely out of it when we got him back. He must remember how Daniella was not only there for him, but also how she stepped up to help him. I remember several instances when she helped Tank clean his wound. It's possible that Cutter remembers that, especially during those early days, before we thought that he was lost to us. So this is weirdly kind of making sense to me right now. Where do you think this is going to go?" she asked.

"No idea, but they left for a walk hours ago, and they've yet to return. So, where did they go? Back to the Widow-maker Lounge to have a drink or two? That's my bet—

because it's too damned cold here to be out in the elements for that long."

"Oh, my God—I totally remember that joint! We used to go to the Widowmaker whenever we had enough money to go to Sugarloaf to ski when we were in college. We used to work our asses off during the week at Pat's Pizza just so we could go."

"We've come a long way, baby."

"And this baby has been put in a corner!" she said. "Jennifer, you have no idea. Harold and Ethel—especially Ethel—are making me feel inadequate on every level. I've got two more days to convince them that I'm the right woman for their son. But I'm telling you, it's like the goddamned inquisition when it comes to those two. Where did I go to school? Oh, a state university, how disappointing because their son went to West Point. Why do I write about zombies? Oh, because I have nothing of substance to say that will better the world. Do I vote Republican? Not so much, which makes them all kinds of cagey. And by the way—as for Ethel? She wants to know whether I know how to bake a proper apple pie—and *that's* where I'm going to hand that bitch her ass, because I *do* know how to make a fabulous apple pie, which she's going to find out tomorrow. I'm going to crush her with my all-American apple pie. I might even put a fucking American flag right in the center of it! Hell, maybe I'll find a Reagan doll while we're here in Lincoln and stick it right beside the flag. And do you want to know what?"

"What?"

"To top it off, I'm going to make my own vanilla ice cream to go along with it. Homemade ice cream with fresh vanilla beans and all of that shit. I am so going to take her down, I can't tell you."

"Is there any way that you could slip each of them a roofie while you're there?"

"Hilarious."

"Just trying for some levity!"

"And I appreciate that. But moving on. How is the house that Alex rented?"

"Beyond beyond."

"Tell me everything."

I told her everything.

"I'm going to sound like a broken record, but God, I wish we were there with you."

"Look, you need to suck it up, sister. You've only got two more days, and you need to use your magic to convince Tank's parents that you're the one for him. So, get with it. Alex and I will spend New Year's Eve with both of you. And who knows—maybe even Blackwell and Marcus will join us. Time will tell —in fact, I have a feeling that tonight is going to be a critical moment between those two. So, we'll see. But just know that civilization is coming your way in a matter of three short days."

"Short?" she said. "Are you kidding me? Ethel knocks on our door at five in the morning singing 'Rise and shine! Breakfast in thirty! Please leave the zombies at the door!'"

"You are so lying about that last part."

"I wish I were, but I'm not. As successful as those books are, Harold and Ethel could give a damn about them because they can't get over that I write about the undead."

"Well, then they're just going to have to accept you for you, because you, my dear friend, are nothing short of a goddamn goldmine."

"Now you sound like Blackwell."

"Maybe so, but she'd agree. I know you're worthy of Tank. All of your friends know that you're worthy of Tank.

And Tank certainly knows it. So, either they're on board or not. If they are by the time you leave—great. But if they're not, don't you dare let that rattle you. I expect you to keep your chin up—do you hear me?"

"I do. And I will. I'm not going to let those two ruin what I have with my man."

"Perfect."

"So, what else have you been doing today? I'm sure that you're going to put on one mother of a Christmas Eve party —which I can't attend! Sadness and woe!"

"Girl, you do need a martini."

"You don't even know, but Tank will soon be my savior when it comes to that. So, answer my question. Take me away from my life."

"Well, when you called, I was putting together a playlist for tonight's party, and I have to tell you—some of the Christmas music was downright depressing, but not necessarily in a bad way. If you know what I mean."

"You were listening to Streisand again, weren't you?"

"You know me too well."

"Like the back of my hand. And that album is so beautiful and so powerful and so depressing, it's enough to sucker punch anyone. I mean, my God—talk about going into a dark hole. Leave it to Babs to take us there. But I love that album as much as you do. After listening to it, you feel as if you want to cut your wrists, but you're also happy that your life isn't as grim as her vocals. I declare it the most fucked up and beautiful Christmas album ever to come from a Jew."

"You did not just say that."

"Well, it's true. She is Jewish, after all—and there is a dichotomy there. And I'm not judging. Thank God she agreed to do that album. With that album alone, Streisand gave to all of us in ways that few ever have."

"It's my favorite Christmas album of all time, but you already know that."

"When we were kids and had sleepovers over the holidays, I remember you sleeping with the album cover."

"You know—I think that I might have."

"You totally did. You hugged it close to your chest as if—well, as if you were holding Alex close to your chest right now."

"I don't think that anyone will ever know just how deeply I'm in love with that man," I said. "Maybe not even you. It's that profound. Is it that way between you and Tank?"

"It is. And I know what you mean. It's so deep that I don't think that anyone would come close to understanding it."

"Thank God we both found a man!"

"Girl, truth!"

"I'm so glad that you called—you've totally lifted my day. I didn't think that I'd hear from you while we were here, but I'm so happy that I did. You must win Harold and Ethel over."

"Oh, girl, game on," she said. "You'll see. I'm in pure tactical mode now. You want an apple pie, Ethel? Your loins are going to get moist when I serve you my pie!"

"That sounds lewd."

"It was meant to. And by the way, Ethel, do you really want someone worthy of your son? Then get ready for me to serve up the prayer at Christmas dinner, because I already have memorized that shit!"

"You're planning on delivering the prayer at Christmas dinner?"

"You're damned straight I am. And if that isn't enough, I

have even more in my arsenal. Like what I'm going to wear at Christmas dinner—totally conservative. Light on the makeup, a longer dress that reveals practically nothing. And then there's how I'm going to be around their son—no touching. No kissing. None of that. I plan on being a total lady. I'm here to win, Jennifer—and I plan to win."

"I love you," I said.

"I love you, too."

"I so wish that you were here with me, because I miss your face. Tell Tank that all of us love and miss him as well."

"I will. And look, this Christmas shit with the potential rents is a one-time deal. Trust me—we will be spending Christmas together next year. You know—when the wedding is behind us. I might have to give Harold and Ethel a Thanksgiving or two, but it's not going to be anything more than that—unless they warm up to me. And that's on them, not me. Because they've hardly been welcoming to me. And this girl is having none of that shit."

"As you shouldn't," I said. "Look, sweetie, I hate to say this, but I need to go. Time is running out. I want to talk more, but there's still so much to do. I'm sorry, my precious one."

"Why are you going all 'Lord of the Rings' on me?"

I giggled when she said that. "Oh, my God—you're right. That wasn't even intentional."

"Well, it spoke to the zombie lover holed up in Prairie Home, NObraska, so you nevertheless scored with that one."

"Yay!"

"Say hello to everyone from me and Tank," Lisa said. And before she signed off, she added: "And ask everyone to pray for both of us. Really hard. I'm talking about getting on their damned knees tonight and praying for us right at their bedside. That's the kind of support we need right now.

Because we do need it, sugar. So, I'll see you in three days. Have a fantastic evening—and don't you dare overlook anything that happens between Daniella and Cutter, not to mention Blackwell and her man. Whatever his name is. Because I'm going to want to hear about all of it!"

"You will. Love you again," I said.

"Love you more."

And with that, my best friend was gone.

It was only thirty minutes later when my SlimPhone rang again. When I pulled it from my pocket, my heart swelled with affection. It was Epifania.

"Epifania!" I said. "How are you?"

"I'm in the Twerks and the Caicos, the cookie," she said. "And Epifania—she the twerking it like she the working it!"

"I can't imagine..."

"Hey, look—I might be alone for the holidays, but Epifania know that it won't be for the long! These cabana boys are the super hot—and one has his eye on me right now for the sure! But enough about him—for the now. How are you and the Alex? I wanted to call and say Merry to the Christmas to both of you, even if it's not officially the Christmas yet. But whatever. Just know that you're on my mind. Where are you now? In Manhattan?"

"No, we're in Maine at Sugarloaf Mountain," I said.

"Well, that sound the super sweet."

"In a way it is. You should see the house that Alex rented for us. It's fabulous. I wish that you could be here with us."

"Oh, the honey, Epifania don't do the cold, OK? She perfectly happy to be soaking up the sun while everyone else is freezing their coochies off."

"Don't you have family you could spend the holiday with?"

"Please," she said. "They just want to go for the Chuckie's money, and Epifania is having none of that! Who are you with, the cookie?"

"Well, Alex is obviously here. And then there's Blackwell and her two daughters. And also Cutter, Brock, and Madison. I believe you've met Madison."

"Yeah, she totally gonna work for me, that one. You'll see. Epifania need to hire a personal assistant—STAT. And she the one who perfect for the yob."

"I'm not sure that you know this, but Madison has received a significant promotion since you first met her."

"Whatever. When I met her, she was Blackwell's assistant. And if that girl was the good enough for her, then she the good enough for me. I'm prepared to triple her salary."

Oh, God...

"How is the weather there?" I asked, wanting to change the subject.

"As hot as the men. You know, ever since I had my little meow-meow tightened, I more confident than the ever. I only been here two days, and already my banging body has attracted a shitload of men. Believe me, the cookie, Epifania plan on having Santa's Christmas sack banging against my little kitty cat later tonight."

I didn't know how to respond to that, so I just said, "Well, good luck with that!"

"No luck needed. Epifania gonna get the laid. But the boy I choose? He needs to be hung. No small prick for this one. Epifania want the big cock."

The loose cannon of Park Avenue truly has no filter...

"How are you even going to know whether he's going to be, uh, you know, as large as you want?" I asked.

"Epifania have her ways," she said. "Even if she needs to pay for a strip and a look, she's totally onboard with that. Because it's the Christmas to the Eve, for the God's sake, and I'm not about to ruin it with something that looks like one of those little pickles I see in the grocery store."

And...we're moving right along!

"Where are you staying?" I asked.

"I bought a house here," she said. "Didn't I tell you that? No? See, that's why I need an assistant! To get the word out! I bought it a month ago, because I love it here. It's this big mother of a house that overlooks the beach. You should see it, Yennifer. So pretty. Views to die for. And plenty of room— you and Alex should come!"

"Well, maybe we will. I've never been to the, uh, Twerks and the Caicos."

"Oh, Epifania would love if you both come. There's plenty of privacy. Over eleven-thousand square feet of it. Some random stud could be banging me in my bedroom, and you'd never even know it. Same for the you and the Alex. You two could totally go at it, and Epifania would never know. Think of this as a safe house for sex. And listen to how smart I am. I made certain that the master bedroom was far and away from all of the other bedrooms. So, you know—no one will ever know when I come or when you come!"

"You're a genius!" I said.

"Please, I'm just a girl from the barrio who got on a rubber boat, got to the States, became a stripper and a maid —and made myself five-hundred million in the process. I still the girl I always been. Street smart, for sure—but no yenius, Yennifer. So, look—this guy keeps checking me out and from where I'm sitting, he looks as if he's hung like a mule. He's wearing this leetle itty bitty white Spandex swimsuit, and holy mother to the God, he's either got balls the size of basketballs, or he's just what Epifania needs to spank her Christmas bells alive tonight!"

"Well, good luck with him—and, you know, all that. Just be careful, OK?"

"Epifania always the careful. It's the men who often leave with the big bruises on their asses because Epifania likes to wallop herself a nice, firm bubble butt. Now, say 'hi' to the everybody for me, OK? Even to the darkness that is the Blackwell. Love you, the cookie. Give Alex a big kiss from me."

"I will."

"Miss you!"

"I miss you, too!" I said, and then I severed the connection. And in a weird way, I did miss her. As crazy as Epifania was, she was as wild as she was good. Sometimes the combination was hilarious. Other times it could leave your jaw on the floor. But her heart was pure, and I was lucky to consider her one of my closest friends.

19

WHEN THE HOUSE was properly decorated and ready to go, it was agreed that all of us would meet in the living room dressed to the nines at seven-thirty—just thirty minutes before Marcus would arrive.

The caterers and servers had arrived on time at six, and from their professional behavior alone, it was clear to me that we were in great hands. So, I just handed over the kitchen to them and left to get ready for the evening with Alex.

When he and I were dressed and ready to go, we appraised each other.

Alex was in a tuxedo that fitted him to perfection. I was wearing a shimmering cosmos-embroidered tulle gown by Valentino. It was a daring choice since it appeared as if I was nude at the torso, but that was just an illusion—and one that Alex clearly approved of.

"Pardon my language, but you look fucking hot," he said when I emerged from the bathroom with my hair straightened and my makeup done up in full force, thanks to Bernie's many lessons.

"Is it too much?" I asked. "I mean, it looks as if I'm baring my breasts, which I'm not. I'm wearing a nude bra, but you really can't tell that I am. Is it too sexy for tonight? I can always change."

"Don't change," he said. "Wear that."

"Well, you certainly said *that* quickly."

"Yeah, because you're turning me on."

"Think about our guests for a moment."

"Why? I want my wife to look like that."

"Alex, I need you to be serious."

"Fine," he said. "Jennifer, since meeting Blackwell, you have turned into a fashion icon in New York. Everyone writes about whatever you're wearing now or whatever you'll be wearing next. You've set a very high bar in Manhattan, and because of that, you've certainly dressed a hell of a lot more daring than this. And everyone here knows that. All of them are expecting you to bring it tonight, and you have. So, have fun with it." And then he cocked his head at me. "Did Blackwell pick that gown out for you?"

"She did."

"Then you'll be getting nothing but applause from your main critic, so relax."

"You know," I said. "I worry about Madison. Here I am wearing a thirty-thousand-dollar gown. Blackwell is going to show up in Chanel—we both know it—and that alone will have cost her a good twenty grand. And then there's Alexa and Daniella, whom Blackwell has clearly set up in ways that are going to make them shine tonight. But Madison doesn't have the means to come anywhere close to what the other women will be wearing, and that bothers me. She's already said to all of us that she's self-conscious about the fact that she 'can't compete' with the rest of us, as if this is a competition, which it isn't—well, at least it isn't for me. I can't say the same for Daniella and Alexa, who are in the weird throes of some sort of unlikely fashion battle. But with that said, I can't blame Madison for how she feels. I hate that she might be feeling inadequate right now."

"Maybe Blackwell and I already have taken care of Madison for that reason," Alex said.

And when he said that, I just looked at him. "What do you mean?"

"That what she'll be wearing tonight wasn't exactly purchased at Century Twenty-One."

"Oh, my God. You've already thought of this? And here is yet another reason why I love you!"

"To be fair, it was Blackwell who thought of it. I just told her to spend whatever she needed to spend to make certain that Madison felt as glamorous as the rest of you girls tonight. When she first came to tell me what she had in mind, it was clear that she was sensitive to the situation. And since I didn't want Madison to feel uneasy when Black-well gave her the gown, which Madison would know had cost plenty, I asked Blackwell to tell her that it was an early Christmas present from the both of us."

"You know," I said as I walked over to him and pulled him in close to me. "When you do things like that, I just want to tear your clothes off."

"Maybe later tonight?"

"In fact, I'm expecting it. It is Christmas Eve, after all. And just so you know, I'm aiming to please."

He kissed me on the neck, and then on the lips. I felt his stubble brush against my cheek, and my whole body tingled because of it.

"Just so you know, I'm aiming to do the same thing to you. Because later tonight, when the party's over, I'm going to have my way with you, Mrs. Wenn. I'm going to bring you to your knees."

"And when I'm down on my knees, don't think that I won't take advantage of the situation. So, get ready for that, Mr. Wenn."

Whenever Alex and I entered into this sort of banter, it became a full-on game between us. Who could one-up the other with the sexy talk before the other one broke into laughter?

"Now you sound like a dirty little tramp," he said with a grin.

I winked at him. "Maybe I am one. Maybe I was born in a red-light district. Maybe I was raised by a gaggle of whores."

That nearly got him, but not quite.

"I think you need someone to take a paddle to that beautiful ass of yours."

I smoothed my hair away from my face, rolled my eyes, and looked bored. "Let me know if you can find someone who has the balls to do it."

"That would be me."

"Then the question is whether you're man enough to use the back of your hand? Because why do you need the paddle? Are you afraid of callouses?"

"Oh, you are so going to get it now."

"Well, not exactly right now—we do have a party to attend, after all. But try to be mindful of this, Mr. Wenn—be careful about how much you drink tonight, because I'd hate to find myself dealing with a limp dick on Christmas Eve…"

The moment I said that, he took my hand in his and cupped it against his cock, which was shockingly rock hard and pulsing in his pants. "I have a feeling that disappointment is out of the question for you tonight, Mrs. Wenn."

"Really?" I locked eyes with him, and then reached down and grabbed his balls. "Well, good. Because I plan to rock each of your snow globes tonight, chickpea. And when I do, I expect a mouthful of tinsel."

His lips wavered a bit when I said that, but still he didn't laugh—damn it!

"You're nothing but a temptress."

"Why even make it sound elegant? I'm a gutter whore."

And that finally did it. Alex reared back his head and howled in laughter.

I lifted my fists above my head. "Jennifer for the win!" I said.

He swept me into his arms. "I'm holding you to all of that, you know?"

"I fully expect you to."

He looked at his watch. "Nearly seven-thirty. We probably should get going."

"Yeah, about that. You're not leaving here with that bulge in your pants. So, you know, think about math or something. Because you are so not walking into that living room with a full-on erection. Daniella alone would totally call you out on it."

"Actually, I'm not sure that she would. Did you see her when she returned from her walk with Cutter? She looked happier than I've seen her in years. And she was polite to everyone—even Alexa. Who's to know what's to come of this?"

"I still can't even wrap my head around what's going on there. Daniella finally landing Cutter? And he instigated it? Yes, on some levels it makes sense to me, but on other levels it makes zero sense. So, I guess we'll see. Now, take a deep breath, think about cows, the color black, and robots or something, because you still need to settle down, big boy."

"It's not that bad."

"The hell it isn't. You're still packing some major heat—and we can't join our guests with you looking like that. So, chill. You can have your way with me later," I said. "And vice versa."

"Now, I'm going to get hard again," he said.

"Then imagine this—your parents having missionary sex on a Victorian bed."

"That did it," he said.

"Good—so, let's go."

WHEN WE ARRIVED in the living room, Streisand's 'Ave Maria' was playing on the Bose surround sound system, candles flickered on tables and on windowsills, the Christmas tree was a towering, heavenly display of glimmering lights, and everyone was there waiting for us, which immediately made me glance down at my watch.

We were, after all, the hosts and should have been here before everyone else had arrived. But we weren't late. Everyone else was either early or on time. It was, after all, seven-thirty on the dot.

"I'm sorry that we're the last ones to be here," I said to everyone as I moved through the group and gave everyone a hug and a kiss on the cheek. "We should have been here to greet you."

"A proper host and hostess would have been," Blackwell said. "Not that either of you know anything about being 'proper'."

"Oh, please," I said as I air kissed her on each cheek. "We're right on time. And by the way, *you're* a knockout tonight. I knew that you'd be wearing Chanel, but I certainly

didn't expect to find you in winter-white. Just look at you
—divooooon!"

"What are you? Six? Seven? Grow the hell up."

"It sounds to me as if somebody hasn't had a cocktail
yet..." I singsonged.

"Actually, none of us have—but to be fair to you, darling,
all of us just sort of happened to come here at once. And
only moments ago—so, you and Alex are good."

"Here come two servers now," Daniella said.

And when she said that, I not only noted that she was
standing next to Cutter, who looked smashing in his black
tux, but that Daniella looked ravishing. She was wearing a
sleeveless, navy blue bead-embroidered gown, with a deep
V neckline that exposed a fair amount of cleavage, but
nothing that could be considered scandalous. The silhouette was fitted and the skirt was straight, which revealed her
body in ways that I knew she wanted it revealed.

"Daniella, you look lovely," I said.

"Thank you, Jennifer. So do you. Your dress is literally
over the moon. Who made it?"

"Valentino."

"Well, there you have it—you pretty much can't go
wrong there. And by the way, I love the way you've straightened your hair tonight. You look as killer as you always do.
What do you think, Cutter?"

"What can I say? When doesn't Jennifer turn it out?"

*OK, so they're totally relaxed in each other's company and
Daniella is clearly going out of her way to be polite and positive,
so what in the hell transpired between them today? Clearly,
something good. And for the lack of drama alone, may it continue!*

"And look at you, Madison," I said. "That dress is a
knock-out." And it was—Blackwell had come through again.
She'd opted for an Oscar de la Renta strapless floral

sequined fit-and-flare dress in ivory that came to just above Madison's knees, which accentuated her long, pretty legs. On her feet was an elegant pair of black Manolo Blahnik BB suede point-toe pumps, which I'd seen for myself at Saks— and which I'd nearly purchased. Looking at them on her now, I kind of wished that I had.

"I love it," she said. "Thank you so much!" She twirled in front of me. "I have no words."

"That's because you don't need any," Brock said, who also was wearing a tux. "You're an exclamation point."

"You two look terrific. I'm really glad that you decided to come along on the trip."

"That means a lot to us, Jennifer," Brock said. "You know, to have your support."

"You have everyone's support."

When I turned my attention to Alexa, she caught me off guard again.

"Oh, my God!" I said to her.

She brightened and then asked, "Do you like?"

"Are you serious? Who are you wearing? It looks like Dior..."

"Actually, it's Dolce & Gabbana. Mom told me what the style of the dress is, but I can't remember."

"It's a black bijoux open-back stretch-crepe dress, Alexa," Blackwell said.

"Right. I'm sure that means something to somebody, but for me, I chose it because it's form-fitting, and because the black matches my hair. And look at the back of it, Jennifer— check out the jeweled bow at the base of my neck."

She lifted away her hair so that I could see it.

"It's insane," I said. "And your back is nearly bare. And hello Christmas, just look at your heels. You've killed it."

"And not one animal was murdered in the making of any

of it—including the heels. Faux leather, not that anyone would know. Still, being a vegetarian and someone who loves animals, wearing something like this is important to me."

"As it should be," I said. "Because that's who you are."

"And by the way," she said. "You look super sexy."

"Believe me, it's all an illusion. Smoke and mirrors. And by the way, everyone, just for the record—my breasts are not exposed! I know that it might look as if they are, but trust me—they're not."

"Well, they should be," Daniella said. "Because you totally could pull it off, Jennifer. I sure wish that I looked like you."

"Why?" Cutter said. "Look at you tonight, Daniella. You're beautiful."

Shit just keeps getting real!

"I agree," Blackwell said. "Jennifer looks lovely, especially since I did, after all, choose that dress for her. And as for the rest of you girls, let's just say that you've made this fashionista proud." She turned to me. "Drinks?" she said.

"Indeed."

ALL OF US were deep into our first drink when the doorbell rang.

"Oh, God," Blackwell said. "That must be him. And what am I to do? How am I to behave? What in the fresh hell have I gotten myself into?"

"Just relax," Alex said as he moved toward the door. "He seems like a nice man. Why don't you just continue to give him a chance? You've got this."

But she didn't, because when Alex opened the door, a

young man was standing just beyond it who was not Marcus Koch.

It took me a moment to place him, but then I recognized him from the night before. He was the cute, twenty-something, dark-haired boy who was the first to approach Alexa at the bar to chat with her the night before. Had she invited him here tonight? She must have, not that I minded. In fact, I welcomed it. With him here and Marcus on the way, all of us would be paired up, which would be perfect.

"Hello," Alex said as he opened the door.

"Hi," the young man said sheepishly. "Is Alexa here? I'm pretty sure she gave me this address, but I never expected to come upon a house like this. I might be at the wrong address. This place is a mansion."

Clutched in one hand was a bouquet of flowers that was still wrapped in plastic, and which made my heart go weak not only because of the gesture, but because he seemed so nervous.

"You're not in the wrong place, Justin," Alexa said as she crossed the room and stood alongside Alex. "Come in out of the cold. Let me take your coat. I'm so happy that you came. Everyone, this is Justin Campbell, *the one I told all of you about earlier. You remember—right?*"

While everyone else just looked at the poor kid with question marks stamped on their foreheads, I immediately jolted into action and walked over to shake his hand before he could figure out that Alexa hadn't shared any of this with any us, likely because she wasn't sure if he'd show—and didn't want to embarrass herself if he didn't.

"Of course we do," I said. "It's nice to meet you, Justin. I remember you from last night. You were the first to talk to Alexa, weren't you?"

"I was—though the other guys I was with tried to steal away her away from me."

"Looks like they lost! And thanks for coming. Merry Christmas Eve. And what beautiful flowers you have. They're lovely," I said.

"They're for Alexa," he said, holding them out to her. "They're not much—it's hard to find a proper florist around here. I would have done better if I could have, but it is what it is—and I hope that you like them, Alexa."

"I love them," she said as she took them. "Thank you."

When she said that, his eyes roamed over her and I thought for a moment that I saw him blush. "You look amazing," he said. "I mean, really amazing. I think that I might have underdressed..."

"I know that suit," Blackwell said as she moved toward him. "Brooks Brothers. Black, but with a festive red vest. You are not at all underdressed, Justin, so think nothing more of it." She held out her hand to him. "I'm Barbara," she said. "Alexa's mother. It's a pleasure to meet you. I'm also happy that you're here."

"Thank you," he said.

"But I have to ask—why *are* you here?" she said. "It's Christmas Eve. Don't you have a family you should be with now?"

Oh, Christ. Blackwell, give the kid a break. Do you really need to be that direct?

"Actually, my parents are kind of in the middle of a divorce," he said. "And it's starting to get heated between them. Since I don't want to be around that kind of negative energy over the holidays, a few buddies of mine decided to come to the Loaf with me so that I could get my mind off all of it."

"Well, then you have the very best of friends, don't you?" Blackwell said.

"In fact, I do."

"I'm sorry for what you're going through. And you are absolutely welcome here—please know that, Justin. Consider us your family tonight."

And when Blackwell said that, the tension I noted on Justin's face and in his shoulders lessened a bit. "Thank you," he said.

As I took his black overcoat from him, Blackwell said, "What do your parents do?"

"My mother is a gynecologist and my father is a brain surgeon."

"They're a what?"

"A gynecologist and a brain surgeon."

"Well, how perfectly perfect," she said, finishing off her martini in one fell swoop. "How divoon. And what do you do, Justin—if I might ask?"

"I'm in my first year at the NYU School of Medicine."

"Then let's get you a drink!" she said. "And let's all have a toast to that!"

"Mother," Alexa said. "How about if I introduce Justin to everyone while you take a chill pill?"

"Fine, fine," she said. "Introduce, introduce."

"In fact," I said, taking Blackwell by the arm. "Could you help me in the kitchen?"

"In the what?"

"The kitchen."

"What's a kitchen?"

"Just come with me, for God's sake."

"Off we go to the kitchen!" she said. "Which I've heard gynecologists, brain surgeons, and young men in medical school tend to use in the preparation of foodstuffs. Of course I'll join you in the kitchen, Jennifer. And we'll talk later, Justin?"

At the very moment that I swept her away him before any further damage could be done, he said that they would.

20

"What in the fresh hell is wrong with you?" I asked when we entered the kitchen, where the caterers and servers were busy at work. "You were a horror show back there."

"Don't blame me!" she said. "I sure as hell didn't know that he was coming. A good-looking man in med school for Alexa? And who hails from *that* sort of pedigree—even if they are divorcing! Please, God, say that it's so!"

"They've only just met. You need to calm down. The worst thing you could do for Alexa right now is scare him away from her, which believe me, I know you have that power within you. So, here are your orders going forward tonight—leave those two alone. Alexa needs to experience this and absorb whatever comes from it, so don't you dare interfere with any of it. Just stay out of it."

"Well, aren't *you* direct?"

"Somebody needs to protect her from you. So, come on, just let them be. OK?"

"Well, fine. I'll 'just let them be'."

"Good," I said. "But he is handsome, isn't he?"

"I could give a goddamn what he looks like. Given what I

know about him now, he might as well look like a troll. What perked me up is finding out that one day he'll be a doctor. *That's* the kind of man that Alexa needs."

"We have another guest," I heard Alex call out.

"Damn," Blackwell said. "It's him—the evil one."

"Why is he suddenly evil?"

"Because he's so damned persistent."

"I think you're just freaked out because you're attracted to him."

"Please—you don't know me that well, girl."

"Like hell I don't. So, come on, let's go and say hello to Marcus. And don't blow it with him. At the very least, give him a chance."

"To what end?"

"Potentially, your own happiness. Now, come on."

"Before we go, how do I look?"

She struck a pose.

"Fantastic, as always. And see—you do care, because you never would have asked me that if you didn't."

"Whatever."

When we left the kitchen and stepped into the entryway, I decided that Blackwell was crazy if she wasn't blown away by how well Marcus was dressed and groomed, because this was clearly him at the top of his game. He had totally stepped it up. He was wearing a tailored black overcoat that came in closely at the waist, emphasizing his broad shoulders in ways that were nothing short of alluring.

As he and Alex exchanged introductions and pleasantries, the overcoat came off, Alex took it from him, and then there was Marcus in what I knew on sight was a Dior Homme suit because Alex had one exactly like it himself. The tie Marcus wore was red, and his thick, graying hair was raked away from his face in ways that were at once masculine and stylish. With his face's chiseled lines and strong, dimpled chin, this man was hot.

"Hello, Barbara," he said when he saw her.

"Marcus," she said as she reached out to shake his hand, which he held for a beat too long. "How good of you to come."

"You look beautiful."

"And yet here I am—wearing nothing more than a mere rag," she said.

His face broke into a smile when she said that, and then he cocked his head at her. "I think we both know better. Did you dress with me in mind?"

"How presumptuous."

"Is it? Because I might have dressed for you."

"An utter waste of time."

"Was it?"

She gave him a full once-over. "The suit," she said. "Dior Homme. And the shoes—custom made, likely in England. Am I wrong?"

"How do you even know that?"

"It's what I do. It's who I am. *Je suis un fashionista.*"

"Then I'm glad that I've dressed properly," he said. "*Parce que je ne voudrais pas vous décevoir.*"

"You speak French?" she said.

"And Italian and Spanish."

"Fluently?"

"*Correntemente,*" he said in Italian. "Or, shall I say, *con fluidez.* Or maybe *couramment...* You know—whichever you choose to respond to."

"The romance languages," she said. "You do speak them..."

"And apparently you respond to them."

"You have no idea."

And when she said that, Marcus Koch leaned forward and kissed her on each cheek. "Take a chance and get to know me better, and you'll find out just how romantic I am."

"*Mon dieu!*" Blackwell said.

Mon dieu, indeed, I thought. But as one of the party's hosts, I needed to check myself and welcome him.

"I'm glad that you came, Marcus," I said as I walked over to shake his hand.

"I had no intentions of missing tonight, Jennifer. Thanks to you and to Alex for inviting me into what I have to say is a beautiful home."

"Oh, this isn't ours," I said. "We just rented it."

"It's still beautiful. I don't know if you've seen the house outside at night with all of the lights on and that enormous Christmas tree in the living room window, but it's stunning."

"Well, thank you. Look, we've already had one round of drinks," I said. "But now with you and Justin here, let's have another." I looked over at one of the servers. "Would you please take everyone's orders?" I asked him.

"Of course," he said.

"And the first serving of hors d'oeuvres can be brought out at any point."

"I'll let the others servers know."

"Thank you," I said. And as he made his way around the group to ask what they'd like to drink, I shrank away from Blackwell and Marcus so they could be alone to talk. I reached for Alex's hand, and we stepped aside to assess the room.

"Well, this is going to be interesting," I said to him in a low voice. "He and Barbara are already talking."

"He seems like a good guy. Good for Blackwell."

"Good for her if she doesn't screw it up. Charles really did damage her, you know? She loved him—and then he cheated on her. Will she let another man in so soon? I'm not so sure, but I hope that she will."

"I guess we'll see."

I turned to look at him. "You do know, my darling husband, that this is either going to be the best party ever—or the worst one in history. It all depends on three factors."

"I have a pretty good idea what they are, but let's hear what you think."

"If Daniella messes things up with Cutter and gets one too many drinks in her, expect a ruinous evening. If Alexa doesn't connect with Justin, well, she might just become sullen and disappointed. As for Blackwell, if she doesn't hit it off with Marcus tonight, I'm not sure what to expect. But I think we both agree that if any drama is going to hit, it's going to come from Daniella. Agreed?"

"Totes."

"You're killing me."

"I said it in honor of Daniella. And just so you know, while you're focusing on all of potential drama that might take place tonight, I'm focused on what I'm going to do to you later."

"Oh, God," I said. "You know that you can't do that to me now. You can't make me become a willing woman in the middle of a party. And in front of our guests, no less. So, check yourself, big boy. Get yourself in line."

"I'll be right in line behind you later tonight."

I just looked at him in exasperation.

"Alex, you know what you do to me when you come on to me like that. It's like the first time I set eyes on you—I turn into a silo of heat. You can't do this to me now. It's not fair."

"Fine," he said as his stubble brushed against my neck, which naturally turned my nipples into a pair of torpedoes.

"Because when it comes to you, Mrs. Wenn, you have no idea what's coming. Or how I'm going to make you come again and again and again tonight. So, you know—brace yourself for that. Because that's how this evening is going to end for you. You think that you know me in the bedroom? Maybe a bit—but tonight I'm bringing all of it. And all I can say is this—good luck walking tomorrow morning, love. Because if you are able to walk, that might just turn out to be your favorite Christmas gift of the day."

21

As THE EVENING WORE ON, cocktails and hors d'oeuvres came out at a steady pace. And since I wanted to leave Blackwell alone with Marcus as much as I could, Alex and I focused on mixing with the rest of the group.

"Let's go over and talk to Brock and Madison first," I said. "I mean, look at them over there, with his arm around her shoulders and holding her in tight. Totally in love. The expressions on their faces remind me of the first time that we fell in love."

"Lead the way," Alex said with his hand on my ass.

"Lift your hand a bit higher, please."

"Not happening."

"Alex, I need to be coherent, and so do you."

"I'm perfectly coherent."

"Well, I'm not. Stop teasing me like this. I'm going to have to change my underwear if you keep this up."

"Oh, I'm so keeping this up," he said. "I'd rather skip all of this and just get you into bed."

"You're terrible. Tonight is about our family and friends."

"Yeah, yeah," he said. "You keep telling yourself that, because you already know better. Later tonight, I'm going to have at you like I've never had at you."

Oh, God... He truly is insatiable.

"You can't talk like that here!"

"Then why are you on the verge of laughing right now?"

"You already know that I get a kick out of it when we talk dirty to each other. But we can't do that here. And we're nearly upon them. So smile, for God's sake. And lift your hand higher."

"Still not happening."

He is incorrigible!

"Hi, guys," I said to Brock and Madison as we approached them. "Merry Christmas Eve!"

"Hi, you two," Brock said. "Great party. Thanks again for inviting us. Madison and I are having a terrific time."

"Our pleasure," Alex said. "I can't remember the last time you and I spent a Christmas together, Brock, but I do seem to remember that we got into some sort of trouble when we did spend Christmases together."

"You and I both know that we did."

"Well, there's that."

"Are you ready to cook that turkey with me tomorrow, Madison?" I asked.

"You have no idea—I'm really looking forward to it! And guess what?" she said. "Brock is going to join us."

"You cook?" I said to him.

"I do. Alex and I both know how to cook because of one special person—right Alex?"

"You've got that right," Alex said.

"Michelle?" I said. "You also learned from her, Brock?"

"I did. Whenever Alex and I hung out together when we were kids, both of us always gravitated toward her. You would have loved her, Jennifer. She really was the best. She wasn't just kind and loving, but she was funny as hell. Michelle taught each of us plenty—and not just about food. But about life. And the real things that matter in life. Is that a fair assessment of her, Alex?"

"She was the mother I never had."

"I know she was, and I'm glad that she was there for you. Because your mother and father sure as hell weren't. But let's talk about none of that tonight. Michelle taught me how to bake, so that's what I'm going to be in charge of tomorrow while you two ladies tend to dinner."

"And the kitchen is massive," I said. "It has two islands, so you can have one for yourself, and Madison and I will take the other."

"Perfect." He shot Alex a look. "Want to join me?"

"We could make Michelle's apple pie..."

"And her chocolate cream pie."

"And her pear clafouti."

"Oh, man, I remember her pear clafouti. It was so good. Do you remember how to make it? I don't, but I remember how to make the other two."

"I remember."

"So, are you in with me on this?"

"I'm all in," Alex said. "It'll just give me an excuse to spend more time not only with my beautiful wife, but also with you and Madison."

"That's kind of what I was thinking, only—you know— with my beautiful Madison."

"Well, then, let's just touch our glasses to that, Madison," I said as I lifted my martini to hers. "Our men think that we're beautiful. And how about that for an early Christmas present?"

"I think my man is one hot, smoking stud," Madison said

in a voice that was oddly deep. "His parents might have called him Brock, but sometimes I call him 'Bronco'."

"You do not," I said to her.

"Hello?" she said. "Six months and going stronger than ever—and there are a whole host of bucking bronco reasons for that. Believe you me when it comes to *that* one..."

"TMI!"

"You can handle it. And just so you know, I see no end in sight when it comes to the two of us, because I am in love with him. More than he probably knows."

She looked over at Brock, and the grin on his face reflected everything that he felt for her and all that was passing between them right now.

"I love you, too," he said.

"And I sense a romantic moment coming on," I said. "So! We'll just scoot and go over to see how Daniella and Cutter are getting along."

"See you tomorrow morning," Madison said. "Gifts first —then the four of us will tackle Christmas dinner!"

"It's going to be epic," I said, and then I kissed each of them on the cheek before Alex and I set off into what was or wasn't going to be a minefield.

"Hello!" I said to Daniella and Cutter.

When we approached them, they were standing next to the Christmas tree, far away from everyone, and deep into conversation. And they were shoulder to shoulder, no less. "Are you having fun? Have the servers been around? You're way over here—I have a feeling that they haven't been anywhere near you."

"They've been wonderful," Daniella said. "And what

they're serving—my God, Jennifer. You and Uncle Alex have outdone yourselves again. Thank you! Everything has been fabulous."

She looked up at Cutter, and I saw nothing but love in that girl's eyes, which concerned me. I certainly hoped that Cutter knew what he was doing, because whatever was taking place between them now would kill that girl should he suddenly pull back.

"What do you think, Cutter?" she asked.

"It's been an amazing evening," he said. "The hors d'oeuvres alone have pretty much been a meal."

"That was the intent," I said. "Since we weren't having a proper dinner tonight, Alex and I wanted to make sure that everyone was still properly fed by a whole host of different little bites. And believe me—the food has only just started to roll out. So, are you two having fun?"

A loaded question, for sure, but with Daniella's heart on the line, it was one that I wanted to know the answer to...

"We're having a great time," Daniella said. "Cutter was just telling me about the time he spent as a soldier in Afghanistan. I never knew about any of that because Cutter is pretty private when it comes to the time he spent overseas. But, Jesus, just listening to his stories—he's a hero. I can't believe what I've heard tonight. I never knew this side of him."

"I have a feeling that serving our country was just as important to Cutter as it was to Tank," I said. "Whom I wish was here with us tonight, along with Lisa."

"It doesn't feel right without them here," Daniella said.

"It doesn't, but it is what it is, I guess. They're planning to get married next year, so she had to meet his parents at some point, and the holidays pretty much made sense —I guess."

"Agreed," Cutter said. "But maybe we'll have them with us next year—after the wedding."

"Lisa has already promised me that we will."

"Well, that's good," Daniella said. "Because I think that all of us are missing them right now."

Who are you? I thought. *What happened to the old Daniella? You not only look beautiful, but you're being perfectly pleasant and well-behaved. Is this thing real between you two? Has he tempered you somehow?* I could only hope that that was the case, but still, I was wary because I didn't want her to get hurt.

"So, what have you two been up to tonight?"

"Well, we've talked a lot about politics given the upcoming election," Daniella said.

Daniella can talk about politics?

"And then there's the state of the world," Cutter said. "We've covered plenty of that. We've talked about race relations, what's going down in the Middle East, and then there's Russia, Syria, ISIS, Turkey, the attacks on Paris and Lebanon, and beyond. There's so much wrong with our world right now, I think it's fair to say that we're living in scary times. We were just talking about the refugee crisis when you came over."

Who is this Daniella? And what have you done with her?

"What's happening right now—on so many levels, whether it comes to the ongoing wars happening around the world, the repeated terrorist attacks taking place here and abroad, or the state of race relations in this country—is dire," I said. "The question is whether you two have sorted it out?"

"That would take several more evenings together," Cutter said. "Which I hope Daniella and I will have."

"Oh," I said abruptly. "I forgot. Cutter, would you mind if

I borrowed you for a moment? On our way over here, one of the servers told us that there's a box in the kitchen that's so heavy that nobody can lift it. Can I steal you away from Daniella for a few minutes so that we can get it out of their way? I have no idea what's in it, but apparently it's too heavy for them to lift."

"Of course," he said.

"We'll be right back," I said to Daniella and Alex, and when I caught Alex's glance, I could tell that he already knew what I was up to. And since he was nothing if not cool, he just breezed right along with my lie and started to talk with Daniella.

When Cutter and I reached the kitchen, I took him aside.

"This has nothing to do with lifting a box."

"I figured it didn't."

"What's going on between you two? You know how that girl feels about you—she's in love with you. She always has been—hell, she even proposed marriage to you, for God's sake, and believe me, she meant it when she did. Look, I know that none of this is any of my damned business and you can shut me down right now if you want to, but I'd hate to see her get hurt if you continue on like this. It would devastate her if you decided to pull away."

"But what if I want to continue on?" he asked.

"Do you?"

"Maybe I do. But we're going to have to get to know one another a lot better first, which I explained to her during our walk this afternoon."

"So, she's fully aware that this might go nowhere?"

"Of course she is. I'm not blind or insensitive, Jennifer— I know how she feels about me. And I thought long and hard before I decided to engage her last night because I'm not going into this with any intention of hurting her. I'm attracted to her."

"You are?"

"She's a beautiful young woman—why wouldn't I be?"

"Because she can be a horror show?"

"Here's the person I've come back to time and again—the one who was there for me on the island. The one who I saw praying for me when it was just the two of us in that hut. The one who sat by my side for hours and held my hand when I was nearly delusional—am I to ignore that just because Daniella can often be a handful? I meant it last night when I said that maybe she needed a real man in her life. Somebody who would treat her well and wouldn't jerk her around. If you look beneath the façade Daniella throws up because she's been burned too many times by too many men, there's a good woman in there. And she's smarter and wittier than I ever thought she was. From our conversations alone, she already has proved that to me today *and* tonight. There's a depth to her that I think no one sees because she's always acting up. But when you get beyond that, and you do see that depth, there's something worth paying attention to there."

"All right," I said with a sense of relief. "So, this is real?"

"It's real."

"I'm sorry. I didn't mean to interfere. It's just that I was concerned."

"You're always concerned about all of us, Jennifer, which is why everyone loves you."

"I just don't want to see her get hurt."

"And I've already told her that I can't promise her that. I've made it very clear that we need to take this slowly, and see where it goes. I've been upfront and straight about that. But let's just get this straight—*I'm* the one who pursued *her* that evening at the bar. And I did it on purpose. I'll say it again—despite how Daniella can come off, I'm attracted to her for lots of reasons that likely nobody understands. I do believe that if a real man got hold of her—like me—all of us would see Daniella at her best. I already have today. You just saw a bit of that a moment ago. There's a lot of love and kindness in her, as difficult as that might be for some to imagine."

"Again, I'm sorry," I said, standing on tiptoe to kiss him on the cheek. "I never should have questioned your judgment. You're one of the best men I know, Cutter. I just sort of freaked out when I saw what was developing between you two, and thought about the ramifications that would come from it if it all went to hell."

"Hey, look, it's understandable."

"So, you like her?" I said.

"I do."

"Was there, like, a spark or something?"

"I felt one during our walk today, when I reached to take her hand. And another one when we went to the Widowmaker, had a drink, and talked for a few hours. And earlier tonight, when I realized that Daniella knows a hell of a lot more about what's happening in this world than I ever would have given her credit for—she surprised me there. So, yeah, there have been a few sparks. At least for me there has."

"I think we both know that it's mutual."

"I hope that it is."

I hooked my arm in his and squeezed his hand. "Sorry for the bullrush," I said.

"Don't worry about it. I'm sure that everyone here tonight has been questioning it. It's not as if either of us didn't expect some sort of reaction. It just means that you care, that's all."

"I hope that you two can come together."

"After the day and evening we've shared, so do I."

"I can't even believe we're having this conversation," I said. "You and Daniella—it just seems impossible to me."

And that's when Cutter stopped me cold. He took me gently by the hands, and just looked down at me.

"There's no timetable for love, Jennifer. Or for attraction to settle in and take hold. Or for a moment to happen between two people that startles them in ways that makes them see each other anew. But I'm here to tell you that it's starting to happen between Daniella and me. And that I'm eager to see where it goes from here. I hope that you and everyone else will support that."

"I do—and if others, like her sister, are resistant to the idea, I'll make sure that minds change."

"And how do you plan to do that?"

I put my arm on his shoulder as we started back toward Alex and Daniella. "Oh, Cutter, my dear friend—and I mean that, by the way, because I do consider you a dear friend—if you think that Blackwell is the only one with a few tricks up her sleeves, then we clearly haven't spent nearly enough time together."

22

LATER, when the evening started to wind down, Alex and I stepped deeper into the living room and took note of who was with whom, which really hadn't changed at all. During the evening, there were times when people mixed, but with three budding new couples getting to know one another, it was nice to see that new connections were being made on a night as meaningful as this.

Alexa and Justin were still talking in ways that were nothing short of animated. Earlier, when Alex and I tried to approach them to say hello, they were in a full-on heated discussion about the state of global warming—what to do about it and what not to do about it—and so we just smiled at them and moved on, not wanting to interrupt them.

Apparently, from the sounds of it, Alexa had found herself a fellow environmentalist.

Daniella and Cutter had taken to one of the sofas near the Christmas tree, and were looking at the glimmering lights and listening to the music while they sipped their drinks. They weren't holding hands, but you couldn't have fit a knife between them if you tried.

As for Blackwell and Marcus, never once did they part.

They had taken to the two leather club chairs at the end of the living room opposite where Daniella and Cutter sat, and Blackwell was so engaged by whatever conversation they were having that she was leaning in to him—nodding, gesturing, or shaking her head in disagreement. Who knows what they were talking about, but what was completely clear to me was that Blackwell was no longer acting up as she had when Marcus first arrived. She was being herself, and she was clearly intrigued by him. And that alone made my night.

Who knew what would come of any of this? It seemed as if this evening had turned into the live equivalent of match.com.

As for Brock and Madison, the second-most senior couple here, we caught them canoodling and laughing throughout the night.

"Total success," I said to Alex as I reached for his hand.

"Couldn't agree more."

"I mean, just look at everyone."

"I am. It's wonderful. And baffling. But still wonderful. If you know what I mean."

"Oh, I get it. It's as if you rented a place for us at Club Med rather than Sugarloaf."

He laughed when I said that and drew me in close to him.

And when he did, I turned to him. "Thank you for this," I said as I wrapped my arms around his waist and kissed him on the lips. "None of this would have been possible without you. You're so kind to everyone, Alex. It's one of the many reasons why I'm madly in love you. I can't tell you how happy I am to call you my own."

"And let me just underscore that—I *am* yours."

I pressed the palm of my hand against his stubbled cheek and kissed him again. "You know, for so many years, I never knew what happiness was. It always was this shining, magical, ethereal thing that forever remained just out of my reach. But look at me now—with you and the family we've built together, I'm the happiest girl in the world. Thank you for not only being my husband, but also for being my best friend. You are my gift this Christmas, and last Christmas, and all of our Christmases yet to come. I'm so grateful for you, Alex. You mean everything to me, and I don't say it often enough. But you do. Don't you see?"

"I do see, and it's humbling. You're the love of my life, you know?"

"I do know, because I can feel it. I feel it when we wake up together, I feel it when we work together, I feel it when you make love to me, and hell, I can even feel it now. How did we ever get so lucky?"

"Those are questions for the universe to answer," Alex said. Then, he took me into his arms and kissed me gently on the forehead and then on the lips. "As for us, we just get to enjoy the rewards."

WHEN THE EVENING was over and all of us had gathered in the entryway, I retrieved Marcus and Justin's coats—and was pleased to learn that both of them would be joining us for Christmas dinner.

"We'd be happy to have you both," I said to them. "Consider our rented house your rented house."

"Thank you, Jennifer," Marcus said. "And also to you, Alex. It was a real pleasure. You know, if you hadn't invited me, I would have spent the night drinking alone and thinking about Barbara."

"The hell you would," she said. "You'd be holding up your glass, happy to be rid of me."

"You know, you do make me laugh," he said to her. "And that doesn't happen often."

"And yet here I stand—nothing if not serious."

But she wasn't, because there was a twinkle in her eye and a trace of a smile on her face when she spoke. Was something really happening between them? Oh, how I hoped that there was. Please, God, give us this Christmas miracle!

"And how about you, Justin? I know that you're here with friends, but we'll be having breakfast tomorrow after we open gifts. You and Marcus are certainly invited to that as well. Would either of you like to come for breakfast?"

"As much as I'd enjoy spending more time with Alexa, I can't let my buddies down," Justin said. "They came here to support me because of the divorce and all. So, for them, I'm going to need to spend the day on the slopes. I hope that you understand." He looked at Alexa. "And that *you* understand."

"Of course I do," she said. "Have fun. I'll see you tomorrow night at dinner."

"And she will," I said. "Your friends must be very close to you to have your back at a difficult time such as this, Justin. Enjoy your time skiing tomorrow—and don't break a leg, because we want you at Christmas dinner, OK?"

"I'll do my best."

He was adorable.

"Breakfast tomorrow, Marcus?" I asked.

"I'm also afraid that I can't make it, though I wish that I

could. Believe it or not, tomorrow morning and afternoon, I need to work."

"On Christmas Day?" I said.

"Managing a hedge fund doesn't ever let up. But I promise that all of that business nonsense will be out of the way and out of my head before I arrive for dinner." He glanced over at Blackwell. "Because I want to be present for that. And also for you, Barbara."

"Don't put this on me," she said. "I eschew your business affairs, and will take no responsibility for any reason why you can't find it in your heart to join us for breakfast tomorrow."

And when she said that, the message was clear—Blackwell was indeed interested in him. She'd just baited him, for God's sake.

"Would you like me at breakfast tomorrow?"

"I'm completely indifferent to what you do or don't do."

He laughed again at her dismissive response, and Blackwell just shot him a look, as if she found none of this amusing. But if you knew her as well as I did—and if you caught the look in her eyes that flashed for only a second—it was clear that she wanted him at breakfast.

"You know," he said. "It's still early enough that I could get a fair amount of work done tonight. And also later in the afternoon tomorrow before dinner. Breakfast would make for a welcomed break, if you'd have me."

"Of course we would," Alex and I said at once.

"You two are so predictable," Blackwell said.

"We'll be opening gifts at seven," I said. "Breakfast at ten. Does that work for you, Marcus?"

"When I'm motivated, I can make anything work."

"Well, how positively alpha of you," Blackwell said.

"Actually, Barbara, you have no idea just how 'alpha' I can be."

"Goodness!"

"Am I in my body right now?" Daniella asked. "I feel as if I'm floating in space and going toward a bright light. How about you, Alexa?"

"I'm right there with you," she said. "Though I feel as if I'm heading toward a black hole—and I'm untethered."

"Anyway," I said. "Then we'll see you at ten tomorrow, Marcus. And believe me, it will be very, very casual."

"Speak for yourself," Blackwell said.

"Fine," I said to Marcus. "That one will probably be dressed in some sort of Chanel couture, but the rest of us won't be, so please feel free to come as you are. It's only for breakfast, for goodness sake."

And it was then that Marcus Koch decided to turn up the heat on Blackwell.

"I'm only going to come if you ask me to come," he said to her.

"If I ask you to what?"

"To come."

"How rude."

"To come for breakfast," he said with a smile, again clearly getting a charge out of Blackwell's sense of humor. "So, you know, invite me or don't."

"Fine. I would like to have you at breakfast. You can low-carb it with the rest of us if you'd like."

"I would like."

"Then I guess we'll see you here at ten," she said.

"I'll see you tomorrow at ten," he said as he came forward and gave her a peck on each cheek.

"Why were your lips just on my cheeks?"

"The question you should be asking yourself is why you leaned into me when I leaned into you? So, tomorrow?"

"Fine—but don't you dare be late. I loathe tardiness."

But as Marcus and Justin moved toward the door and opened it, Marcus turned to her just before he left. "I won't be late. So, good night. And sleep tight—if you can."

And with that, he closed the door shut behind him, and I just looked at Blackwell, who had all eyes on her.

"It's time for bed," she said. "I'll see all of you horrible, gaping, awful people in the morning. What a horrific evening. I mean, really! The presumption of that man. Apparently, it knows no bounds."

She started to walk away from us.

"Well, it couldn't have been that bad," I said. "You did, after all, invite him to breakfast and to dinner."

When she stopped and turned to look at me, she leveled me with a glance, but she nevertheless overlooked my comment, which was telling in and of itself. "Alex and you will try your best to keep it down for the rest of us tonight, won't you? Yes? No? Improbable? Or is it impossible? Either way, shut your doors, try not to be selfish, and bury your faces into your pillows whenever the need arises. Because some of us need our sleep. Understood? Good. Now, enough of this. Good night!"

23

LATER THAT NIGHT, when the evening was over and our guests had left, the rest of us gave each other a hug before we retreated to our bedrooms—where Alex clearly had ideas of his own.

"Close the door," he said. "You know, like Blackwell asked. To be fair, it's probably not a bad idea, given what I'm about to do to you."

And what are you about to do to me...?

A shot of adrenalin rushed through me as he dimmed the lights, and I shut the door and turned to face him.

"Take off your dress," he said.

"Take off your suit."

"Always my equal," he said.

"Always."

"But not tonight. Tonight, what I want for Christmas is for you to give yourself completely to me, and by that, I mean for you to let me take charge. Because I want to take charge. That's my Christmas wish—for me to do everything, and for you to do nothing but what I ask of you. I told you that I'm going to make you come so many times tonight that when I'm through with you, you're not going to know where you are or even who you are. Will you give that to me?"

Giving up control on any level—especially when it came to my body—was never in the cards for me. But this was Alex, the man I loved and trusted implicitly. He would never hurt me—in fact, I knew that his intent was only to give me pleasure. To watch me writhe and moan beneath his touch.

So, I agreed.

"I'll give that to you," I said.

"Then, take off your dress."

I took it off as he removed his jacket and tie, and opened the buttons at his throat so that his shirt parted, revealing his lightly hairy chest. Then, he sat down on the chair at the end of the bed, spread his legs wide open, and casually rested one of his hands on his crotch.

"Now, your bra."

I removed it.

"Give it to me."

I tossed it at him, and he snatched it with ease. "Now, your panties. But don't throw them at me this time. Instead, come over here and hand them to me."

I did as I was told, and when I stood naked before him and gave him my panties, I saw the desire on his face. He held them up to his nose, breathed in my scent, and then dropped them at his side as he stood up and took me into his arms. When he did that, I could feel the full length of him pulsing against my thigh.

"You're so fucking beautiful," he said to me. "I don't think I'll ever be able to get enough of you, Jennifer."

Before I could respond, he dropped to his knees, his mouth pressed against my sex, and his tongue entered me in ways that were so powerful, I had to steady myself by putting my hands on his shoulders. His tongue swirled inside of me—dipped and retreated from me—and the only thing that I could do was close my eyes, arch back my head, and give myself over to him. I gripped the back of his hair and moved his face even closer to my sex, but he was having none of that, because he'd already told me that he was in control.

"Get on the bed," he said.

I got on the bed and watched him slowly take off the rest of his suit—layer by layer. First his shirt, shoes, and socks. And finally his pants so that he was standing before me in a tight-fitting pair of black Dolce & Gabbana shorts. He cupped his hardness in his hands, shook it, and cocked his head at me. "You want this?"

"Is that even a question?"

"In fact, it is. Do you want it?"

There was a new note in his voice—a domineering note. Was he about to go all *Fifty Shades of Grey* on me? I hadn't read the book or seen the movie, but I certainly knew what they were about—domination. Could I handle something like that, if that's what he even had in mind?

Since I did trust him, I simply said, "I do want it."

"How bad do you want it?"

He was getting me so horny, I just told him the truth. "I want you inside of me. I want you to fuck me."

"Which hole?"

What the hell?

But instead of answering, I pushed myself back on the bed, spread my legs, and hoped for the best.

And it was the best.

I was wet when Alex mounted me, and for the next two hours, he did indeed have his way with me. Because this evening was the only gift he'd asked of me, I was complicit through all of it, and I have to say that allowing him to have complete control of my body—and my pleasure—was liberating in ways that we'd never explored.

Why hadn't I let myself go like this before? What had held me back? My urge to retain my own control? If that was the case, then I needed to lose it more often, because this was amazing.

Together, we became a collision of sex, with Alex putting me through the motions with an effortlessness that was so confident and assured, it was beyond sexy. He laid me on my back, and drove into me. He turned me on my side, came up behind me, and thrust into me until I screamed out as I came. Not satisfied with that, he stood above me, lowered his cock into my mouth, and released himself into me with a fierceness I'd never seen in him before.

"Come over here," he said. He was standing at the end of the bed by the wall of windows, which overlooked a night sky filled with a blanket of shimmering stars. Somehow, he was still rock hard and throbbing, his heavy cock jutting in front of him. He was so lean and muscular from his daily trips to the gym that he looked like a God to me. "Come on," he said. "Against the window."

"So, we're doing this again?" I asked. "We've already done this before. At home. Don't you have anything better to offer me?"

"Are you questioning me?" he said. "Because you shouldn't, Jennifer. Now turn around and face the glass."

I did, and with a swiftness that surprised me, he lifted my left leg high into the air until my heel pressed against the glass. His hands reached around to pinch one of my nipples, and then he started to ram into me in ways that were so brutal and thrilling, I trembled with pleasure as my right cheek pressed against the glass.

"You want to come again, don't you?"

If I was being myself, I would have challenged him and said, "Just try to get me there." But by fully letting myself go and giving everything to him, it allowed him to bring out things in me that even I didn't know existed. "Make me come," I said.

"Not quite yet."

He thrusted even harder into me, his size making me catch my breath. Alex was heavily hung—not just in length, but in girth; he was nearly as thick as my wrist. When he rammed into me like that, even to this day, it still was something of a shock to me.

But a pleasurable one.

All night long, he'd been promising me that I'd see another side of him tonight. And he was correct—he was being rougher with me than usual, but in ways that were exhilarating because he knew exactly what he was doing. And then there were the times when he became more gentle and loving than he'd ever been with me. He awakened my senses with his lips, fingers, and tongue. He drew things out of me that could only have happened with complete trust, which I had in him.

And in the end? After countless positions? Alex came through with his promise. I came five times, while he only came twice.

When we were exhausted and our lovemaking was over, he took me in his arms, carried me to our bed, and laid me on my left side—which was my favorite side for sleep. As he came up behind me, I felt his softening cock press against my ass, and then he held me close to him, murmuring in my ear how much he loved me until I faded into the night, asleep in his arms.

24

THE NEXT MORNING, Alex woke me by cuddling up next to me and kissing me on the neck.

"Merry Christmas, love," he said.

I turned to face him with a smile. "Merry Christmas, Mr. Wenn."

"How are you feeling this morning?"

"Totally relaxed. And maybe completely spent."

"Still sleepy?"

"A bit, but we need to get a move on so we're not late. We're supposed to meet everyone at the tree at seven to open gifts."

"You know, I know of a way to wake up really quickly."

"Why does that sound ominous...?"

"Don't worry—it's harmless."

And with that, he pressed something so chilly against my bare back that I shot up in bed with a yelp and gathered the covers around me.

"What in the holy hell was that?" I asked.

Since neither of us had bothered to dress when we went

to bed last night, Alex was still naked when he said, "Close your eyes."

I narrowed my eyes at him. "What are you up to?"

"Would you close them, please? And no peeking."

And then I knew. With a rush of anticipation, I closed my eyes, and knew from last year alone what was to come—my first gift from him, and one that he wanted to share privately with me. I felt him move about the bed as if he was kneeling in front of me, and then he said, "OK—you can open your eyes now."

And when I did, I saw that what he was holding in his hands was an extraordinary white box of some sort. It looked as if it had been hand-crafted out of some sort of translucent stone-like quartz. I just looked at Alex, questioning him with my eyes.

"It's a one-of-a-kind jewelry box from Harry Winston," Alex said. "I wanted you to be its owner."

"One-of-a-kind?" I said. "It's stunning. I don't think I've ever seen anything quite like it. And it looks heavy."

"It's a bit hefty," he said as he gently turned it around in his hands so that I could have a proper look at it. "See the latticework on the top of the case? And the box's emerald-cut silhouette? I first read about the case in the *Times* a couple of years ago, and when I was deciding what to get you for Christmas, I remembered that article and the box. So, I went to Harry Winston and convinced them to sell it to me—even though it wasn't for sale. Let's just say that they were properly persuaded to part with it."

"Can I hold it?"

"In a minute you can. First, how about if you open it? Because your other gifts are inside..."

When I unlatched the gold clasp on the front and lifted the lid, I was faced with two things—a gorgeous diamond wreath necklace, and cascading diamond earrings that were to die for.

"Oh, my God," I said. "That necklace is iconic."

"You recognize it?"

"Yes, Blackwell and I have commented on it many times when we've been to Harry Winston." And then I looked at him. "Did she have a hand in this?"

"This is all me."

"Alex," I said.

"There's nothing to say. They're for you, Jennifer. They're for the moment we first met in that elevator, they're for the fact that you are my best friend and my wife, they're a symbol of my love for you, and they're for the past year, which we fought through together and won with our friends. There isn't a day that I don't tell you that you're the love of my life, but somehow that never seems enough to me. And while I tried to capture what I feel for you with these diamonds and this box, what you need to know is that even they don't express just how much I'm in love with you. But they do sparkle like you, and because of that, they do remind me of you. So, Merry Christmas," he said. "I love you."

I leaned forward and kissed him deeply on the lips. Then, I put my hand on the base of his neck, and for a moment, we just pressed our foreheads together and soaked each other in.

"You're too good to me," I said.

"You deserve more."

"And yet all I've ever wanted is you. Just you."

"And you have me."

After giving me another kiss, which somehow was even more passionate than the last, he held out the box to me. "Have a good look inside, because they are kind of pretty."

"The understatement of the decade."

"Which do you like best?"

"Everything, including the box. I've never seen anything like it. It looks as if it was crafted from a solid piece of quartz."

"Good call, because it was." He touched the necklace with his finger. "I think this is my favorite," he said. "But since the earrings match, I bought those as well."

I looked down at the necklace and admired it. It was comprised of round brilliant, pear- and marquise-shaped diamonds set within minimal metal at varying angles, which resulted in a cluster of remarkable color and fire.

As for the earrings, each had a total of twelve marquis, pear-shaped and round brilliant diamonds that were suspended on delicate platinum wires, creating the illusion that each stone was floating effortlessly when worn. At this point in my adventures with Blackwell and with my own growing jewelry collection, I knew a few things about diamonds—and I knew that right now, I was looking at over one hundred carats worth of them.

"I'd try them on now, but after last night, I should probably shower first."

He laughed when I said that, and then he kissed me again. "Last night was something," he said.

"Last night was the only gift I needed from you. You didn't have to do any of this, Alex. Don't you know that you're enough? Haven't I made that clear to you?"

"You have," he said. "But this has been a rough year for us in other ways, too. It needed to end like this. It needed to end on a high note of promise and happiness for both of us. I'm telling you that it did."

And when he said that, I knew that he was talking about the loss of our child. The thought of it nearly made me tear up, but I didn't. Instead, I chose to be strong for us, and simply agreed with him. "But we got through it," I said. "Didn't we? It was hard, but we did it. When it comes to us, here's what I know is true, Alex. And I've known it for a while, but now the feeling is stronger than ever."

"What's that?" he asked.

"That there's nothing that we can't get through together, and that there's so much more to look forward to as the years pass by. We will have a family. We will achieve all of our dreams. And we'll be together for the rest of our lives."

"We will," he said.

"I already know that we will. Now," I said. "While my presents are downstairs for you, I do have one gift for you up here."

"You do?"

"I do. Could you put the box on the bedside table?"

"Sure."

And the moment he did, I surprised him by throwing myself on top of him, tossing the covers over us, and then snaking my way down his naked body in a blizzard of tiny kisses until I found what I was looking for.

When I grasped him in my hand, he was already hard.

"Merry Christmas!" I said.

And with that, I happily had my way with him.

25

THE REST of the day was nothing short of a blur.

After all of us met in the living room at seven, we each said "good morning" to each other, grabbed mugfuls of coffee in the kitchen, and took our places on the chairs and sofas that surrounded the tree.

For a moment, I just looked around at everyone before we began to open our presents.

Daniella was sitting on a love seat next to Cutter, who had his arm draped casually over her shoulder; Madison was sitting on Brock's lap in one of the comfortable, over-stuffed leather chairs; Alexa was sitting on one of the sofas next to Blackwell—who already was in a lovely red Chanel suit and fully made up, unlike the rest of us—and Alex and I were on the sofa opposite them. Before us, the tree twinkled and glittered—and outside, it was snowing at a fierce pace.

"Does anyone know how much snow we're supposed to get today?" I asked. "I didn't even know we were going to get snow. We have guests coming."

"We're on a goddamned mountain in the farthest outreaches of the galaxy, otherwise known as Maine," Blackwell said. "Snow is to be expected here. If Marcus or Justin aren't man enough to find their way here today, then I say to hell with them."

"If you don't want Marcus here, fine," Alexa said. "But I'm still hoping that Justin comes. He's not only sweet, but also super smart."

"He'll be here, Alexa," Daniella said. "That boy has his eyes on you."

"Do you think so?"

"Hello? You looked amazing last night and he was mooning over you. If he has to get here by snowmobile, believe me, he will. You've rocked him to his core."

"I hope so," she said. "We have a lot in common."

"And he's in med school, no less," Blackwell said.

"He's more than just his education, Mother. Somehow, he's every bit as invested in saving the environment as I am."

"A match made in heaven," Daniella said. "And by the way, Alexa, I think I need to apologize to you. I'm sorry for always calling you a lesbian, because—from what I've seen this weekend alone—you clearly aren't one."

"That's always been true for me, Daniella, but it's not as if there's anything wrong with being a lesbian."

"I agree! I'm just saying, you know, that I'm sorry."

"Thank you," she said. "And Cutter, keep doing whatever you're doing to her, because this Daniella? This Daniella I actually want to be around."

"I've done nothing but talk with and listen to her," he said. "Sometimes, people just need an outlet so they can become the best person they can be." He put his hand on her knee. "And sometimes, when you least expect it, that person can even catch you off guard."

Oh, my word—what in the hell is happening? Daniella and

Cutter? And Daniella actually just apologized to her sister? May her transformation continue!

"Did everyone have a good time last night?" I asked as I watched—transfixed—as Daniella put her hand over Cutter's.

"We certainly did," Madison said.

"Last night was great," Daniella said. "Thanks for going to all of that trouble, Jennifer and Uncle Alex. It was magic."

"You're welcome, Daniella. It was our pleasure."

"It was totes to the max," Cutter said.

I just looked at him as Daniella rammed her elbow into his side and he laughed.

"Are you mocking me?" she said.

"Maybe."

"Fair enough—but at least you did it well."

With Marcus coming for breakfast, we needed to focus, so I clapped my hands.

"Let's get to the gifts! With the caterers coming at nine to serve breakfast at ten, we have less than two hours to get through all of this. So, let's do it!"

IT WAS at that point that the day's blur really left its exclamation point.

There were too many presents, which ranged from dresses, pajamas, shoes, jeans, tops, sweaters, and jewelry for the girls; to a sweetheart diamond necklace from Brock to Madison, who immediately hugged and kissed him for it; and then a black Dior suit that Alex and I had purchased for Blackwell, because frankly, I thought that she needed to change things up a bit. It couldn't be Chanel all of the time.

"What is this?" she said as she held it up in front of her.

"You know damn well what it is," I said.

"Dior? That's lesser than Chanel. Why is my day already starting to turn dark around the edges? Dying would be the only reason to stop wearing Chanel. But even then, it's in the will—Daniella and Alexa are supposed to bury me in it. Otherwise, they'll get disinherited."

"Just so you know, lovecat, I had that suit made for you."

"Made for me?"

"It was designed specifically for you. There is no other one like it in the world."

And when I said that, her eyes brightened. "You mean—this isn't off the rack?"

"Do you really think I'd ever dare to buy you something that was off the rack?"

"Of course you would. You hail from the bowels of Maine, for God's sake. Who knows when your sordid roots will spring up and try to leach the life out of me?"

"That suit you're holding is an original couture design made only with you in mind. Last August, I started working with one of the senior designers at Dior on it. As in four months ago. I sketched out the original drawing, and then he and I collaborated to improve upon it. And now it's yours."

"Oh, snap!" Daniella said.

"Well," Blackwell said, clearly taken aback and surprised. "I had no idea. You did this for me? You actually reached out to Dior for an original creation that only I will have?"

"And I went a step further. Open the other box that's at your feet."

When she did, she pulled out a pair of black strapless Dior shoes that also were made specifically for her.

"I've been working on those since last July. And I might have also sketched out the design for those."

She dangled the shoes in front of her and admired them. "Well, I don't know what to say other than that they're absolutely divoon. You outdid yourself, Jennifer. I mean, God. Naturally, I've worn couture before, but never anything that was designed specifically with me in mind. And I have to say, my darling girl, that you nailed it. I can't imagine the trouble you went through to make this happen, so thank you. *J'adore*. I'll wear the suit and the shoes tonight at dinner, assuming that they'll fit."

"I know your size as well as I know my own name. Believe me—everything will fit."

And onward we rolled until there were only two other presents left beneath the tree, which I'd made certain would be given out last. One was for Alex from me, and the other was to Cutter from Alex.

"Cutter," Alex said, pointing to the deep blue box adorned with the silver bow. "That one is from me to you."

"Here, let me get it for you," Daniella said, reaching for the gift and handing it to him. "Who knows what it will be?" she said. "Maybe it's a bronze star, because you certainly deserve one after what you did for us on that island."

"I was just doing my job," he said.

"You went above and beyond your job," Alex said. "So, you know—go ahead and open your gift. I chose it myself."

Cutter opened the package and pulled out a Royal Oak Concept Laptimer Michael Schumacher watch, which was as masculine as it was handsome.

"Oh, my," Blackwell said. "Well deserved, my dear boy. A Michael Schumacher—I recognize it on sight. And at a cost of a quarter of a million, no less. Wear it with pride, because my daughter is correct—you earned that watch after what you did for us."

Cutter turned the watch over in his hands, and then he looked over at Alex.

"If this watch is that expensive, you know that I can't accept it," he said. "I appreciate the gesture, Alex, but I was on the job at the time. It was my duty to do what I did. It would be unethical of me to accept this for that reason."

"No, it wouldn't, because you went above and beyond your job. Tank told you that the plane was about to blow. He told you not to go anywhere near it, and still you put your life on the line and fought on. Everyone in this room who was on that island knows that you smashed through the boundaries of your job. So, I won't hear another word of it— that watch is yours. And just to put this into perspective, Cutter, you saved several lives on that island, while I'm only giving you a watch. What I need you to know from my heart is that we are grateful for all that you did for us, and continue to do for us. So, please—accept it without another word."

"All right," he said. "And thank you, Alex. I never expected anything like this."

"And I never expected any employee of mine to step up in the ways that you did for me, my family, and our friends, so thank you again for that."

"Try it on," Daniella said. "It's kind of sexy. Alexa and I went to see 'Spectre' last week, and it kind of reminds me of something that James Bond would wear."

"I can see that," Alexa said.

"It's great looking, that's for sure," Cutter said. When he removed his own watch and replaced it with the Michael Schumacher, he held out his wrist and turned it slowly from left to right. "It's heavy," he said. "Which I like. It feels substantial. And check out the gears, Daniella—you can see pretty much all of them."

"It's like a puzzle," she said. "But one that's been revealed."

"And now for Alex," I said.

"But you've already given so much this morning," he said. "From the suits to the shoes—and, Jesus, to everything else in between."

"And yet I might have saved the best for last. Daniella, would you mind reaching for that last package and handing it to Alex?"

"Of course not."

When she gave it to him, I shot Alex a look of anticipation. "What does one give a man who has everything? Let me tell you *that's* been no small challenge. But I think I might have met it. So, you know, open your gift."

As he did, I held my breath and hoped beyond hope that he would like what was inside.

"What are these?" he said when he lifted the top off the box and looked inside.

"The fanciest cufflinks I could find. I know how you love to wear them, but you've got nothing even remotely close to anything that look like these."

"Well, let's see them, for God's sake," Blackwell said. "What do they look like?"

Alex lifted one of them from the box, and the women in the room swooned.

"They're a pair of Fonderie 47 transforming cufflinks designed by Roland Iten," I said. "There are only twenty in existence."

"They kind of look like a watch," Alexa said.

"Good eye, Alexa—Fonderie 47 makes watches. These are the easiest cufflinks in the world to use. You just need to slip them over the cuffs of your sleeves and clasp them as if you were putting on a watch."

"And you found these without my assistance?" Blackwell said.

"I am capable of finding a gift for my husband."

"Apparently," she said. "And I have to say that they're beautiful. Very masculine. Very now. What are they made of?"

"Eighteen carat rose and white gold—as well as metal from an AK-47 assault rifle."

"As well as a what?"

"You heard me."

"Cool," Cutter said.

"But I don't understand," Blackwell said. "How can that even be?"

"Here's the deal," I said. "And listen up, Alexa, because you're especially going to get a charge out of this. When I purchased them, I was told that the sale would go toward raising funds for organizations that actively destroy guns in Africa, where they often are used to murder women and children."

"I'm loving this already," Alexa said.

"I thought that you would. The sale of just one pair of these cufflinks is enough to fund the purchase and destruction of one hundred assault rifles in Africa. From what I've read about the company in the *Times*, that claim is true. Fonderie 47 has actively destroyed over two-thousand assault rifles by selling just twenty pairs of these cufflinks. I know that doesn't sound like a lot, but it's something, and through its many other products, the company has banished an additional thirty-thousand AK-47's from Africa. So," I said to Alex with a kiss on his lips, "I hope that you like them, on all levels."

"I love them," he said. "And you. Thank you."

"There's something else in the box..." I said. "Just beneath the tissue paper."

He whisked the paper aside, and when he did, he paused when he saw what was inside.

"Well, what is it?" Blackwell asked.

"It's an antique key," he said. "One that's been inlaid with rubies..."

"Might we see it?" she said.

He removed it from the box, held it in the palm of his hand for a moment, and then showed it to the room.

"It's beautiful," Madison said. "But what is it?"

"It's the key to my heart," I said. "All dressed up in red."

"Oh, brava, my dear," Blackwell said. "Well done, indeed!"

"You see, this is why I love you," Alex said. "Who would have thought of doing something as meaningful and as unique as this? I think that this is my favorite gift you've ever given to me—beyond your love."

"Now I'm going to cry," Daniella said.

"Cry on Cutter's shoulder," I said. "Meanwhile, I'm going to kiss my man."

And when I did, Blackwell instructed everyone to just look away before "you catch on fire from the sheer sordidness of it all!"

26

BREAKFAST WAS A FEAST, and it went off without a hitch. Marcus came and continued to casually tease and flirt with Blackwell, who was nothing if not flustered by it. Then, when the meal was over and Marcus was gone, Madison took me by the arm.

"It's nearly noon," she said. "We've got a meal to make."

"Indeed, we do. Let me grab Alex while you get Brock."

"He's already in the kitchen."

"Then you're a step ahead of me. We'll be there in seconds!"

And we were. After I asked Daniella and Alexa to set the dining room table for us—under Blackwell's supervision— Alex and I joined Madison and Brock in the kitchen, where the caterers had left food for a proper Christmas dinner purchased from a list I'd given them earlier.

"Good God," Alex said as he looked into the refrigerator. "How much food do we need?"

"You and Brock can just overlook our twenty-pound turkey and everything else that's in the fridge. Just focus on your pies, because Madison and I will tend to the rest."

"Beyond the turkey and the stuffing, what are you two making?" Alex asked.

"Roasted carrots, the Contessa's gravy, and her potato and fennel gratin. Since Alexa is a vegetarian, she can enjoy the carrots and the gratin, but she needs more to eat than that, so we're making her a killer wild mushroom risotto with parmesan cheese."

"Alexa eats dairy?"

"She does."

"That sounds great," Brock said.

"How about you two?"

"Alex and I are going to make Michelle's apple pie, her chocolate cream pie, and her pear clafouti."

"And that sounds decadent," I said. "So, let's get to it."

"Brock," Alex said. "You know what to do."

"The dough."

"That's right—you're better at it than I am. I'll start peeling the apples."

"We can't disappoint," I said as I hauled the turkey out of the fridge and set it on one of the two islands.

"We won't," Alex said. "The four of us have each other's backs. We've got this."

AND WE DID.

An hour into making the dinner, we were making great progress, so much so that all of us felt comfortable enough to get out of our heads and actually talk to one another. We'd been so focused on what needed to get done, none of us had said much of anything to one another that didn't have to do with cooking the meal.

"How's it going with the gratin?" I asked Madison.

"It's looking good."

"It smells amazing. And this Maine girl has been watching you—clearly, the ladies from Wisconsin know how to cook."

"It's practically been drilled into us."

"And look at me," Brock said. "The happy recipient."

Madison blew him a kiss when he said that while I focused on her dish.

She really was an excellent cook. She'd used a mandolin to slice the potatoes at exactly the right thickness, sautéed the onion and the fennel until they were just tender, and shredded the Gruyère cheese in one of the Cuisinarts. Now, after mixing all of the ingredients with heavy cream, salt, and pepper in a giant bowl, I watched her pour the lot of it into an enormous white baking dish that would serve all of us.

"Damn this bowl is heavy," she said.

"Do you need some help?" Brock asked.

"Maybe later tonight, I will," she said.

"You two are killing me," I said.

She giggled at that, and then pressed down everything into the baking dish before finishing it off with several handfuls of more Gruyère.

"Done!" she said.

"And well done—it looks perfect."

"Now for the carrots," she said after she'd washed her hands.

"Behind you in the fridge."

"Got them. And then the risotto, which really needs to be made at the last minute."

"It does," I said. "Otherwise—sheer ruin."

"By the way," Madison said. "Did any of you notice how tense Blackwell seemed at breakfast this morning?"

"I did," I said.

"Same here," Alex said. "I don't think she knows what to make of Marcus."

I looked over at him. "I think it goes deeper than that—I think she doesn't know whether she can trust another man after Charles."

"Marcus seems like such a great guy," Madison said as she started to cut the carrots on the diagonal. "He's smart, he's successful, he's charming, and he's handsome. Beyond that, he really seems to like her. It was subtle this morning, but that man was flirting with her."

"And Blackwell wasn't herself," I said. "Last night, they talked for hours. And while they still talked throughout breakfast, I could sense a shift in her. Is she second-guessing this? I'm not sure. I don't know how this is going to turn out."

"Let's just hope for the best," Alex said.

"Agreed." I looked over at Madison. "So, when are you and Brock going to move in with each other? It's about time, isn't it?"

"Ummm..." Brock said.

"Too soon?" I asked.

Before he could respond, someone's cell rang. All of us looked at each other, but then Madison held up her hands and reached for her phone in her pants pocket. She looked down at the name on the screen and immediately smiled. "It's Rhoda!"

"I love Rhoda," Brock said.

"Isn't she your clairvoyant friend?" I asked.

"She is—and I adore her. She's my closest girlfriend in the world. I'll make this very quick." She answered the phone. "Rhoda!" she said. "Merry Christmas! I was going to call you after we'd finished making Christmas dinner.

What's that? You want me to put you on speakerphone? Why? Well, you certainly sound bossy today. OK, you're now on speaker. All of us can hear you—so speak."

"Hi, everyone," she said. "And Merry Christmas! Alex and Jennifer, we haven't met yet, but this is Rhoda, Madison's best friend and roommate—in that order."

"How do you even know that Alex and I are here?" I asked.

"A question for the universe. But before we get into the reason for my call, let me save you from what will become an absolute disaster if you don't listen to me, Jennifer. That oven you're working with might be a fancy Viking, but it runs hot. Turn down the temperature from 375 to 325. Cook the bird for four hours, and then cover it with foil for thirty minutes so it can rest and reabsorb the juices. Trust me—if you do that, you'll be sending me flowers tomorrow, because that Butterball of yours will carve as if it's softened butter."

"Do whatever she says," Madison said. "Because she's never wrong when it comes to things like this."

"Thank you, Rhoda!" I said.

"My pleasure. Now, listen to me. Let's just get right to the bottom of the reason why I'm calling. Jennifer, it will be a full nine months before Madison leaves me for Brock. Until then, she still will live with me. And thank the universe for that, because as happy as I am for her and Brock, it's going to kill me to see her go. I plan on treasuring the rest of our time together."

"How do you know that Jennifer just asked that question?" Alex asked.

"Because it's the burden I've been born with, Alex. And by the way—love the cufflinks Jennifer gave you, but it was the key inlaid with rubies that filled my heart and made me pour myself an early glass of wine."

"Holy shit!" I said. "She is the real thing."

"She's got it like that," Madison said.

"I have to say that I'm kind of disappointed, Rhoda," Brock said. "I was hoping that Madison and I would be moving in sooner than that."

"Not happening. She's mine for the next nine months—so cool your heels, big boy. She'll be yours in September. And then you're going to have me on your doorstep every other day."

"I wish that you were here with us now," he said.

"While I'd love to be with you and especially to meet Jennifer and Alex, Alexa, Blackwell, Daniella, and Tucker—"

"It's actually 'Cutter'," I said.

"I'm terrible at names—just ask Madison. I hardly ever get them right. And, man—when it comes to those two? Well, I'll just keep mum about that. Anyway, my business is booming right now. It always goes crazy this time of year, and Mama needs to make the money. I'm closed today, but what a past few days I've had—one customer right after the other, and with the same questions I get asked right before Christmas hits. 'Does he love me?' 'Does she love me?' 'Should I get her the ring now—or later?' 'What will his parents think of me?' 'What will her parents think about me?' 'Can you tell me the Powerball numbers? Because look, psychic woman, I really need some jack.' And that's where I draw the line—I always know the damned numbers, but giving them out would be cheating and unethical."

"I have to meet you," I said. "We must do lunch!"

"Girl, it's already on my calendar," Rhoda said. "Madison is going to introduce you to me on January 14th. We're going to db Bistro, where you used to work before you decided to give Alex a second chance—and look at how well that turned out. What a powerful love story you two share. You know, in a few short years, my Barry is coming to me, and I can tell you that I already know in my heart that he's going to sweep me off my feet just as Alex did to you."

"Rhoda," I said, "if you can find a man like that, then you must do exactly what I did—marry him."

"Oh, toots, that's such a done deal, I can't even tell you," she said. "Barry and I are going to have one hell of a romance! Now, get back to cooking, kids. Madison, I love and miss you like crazy. Brock, I also love you—take good care of my girl for me. Alex and Jennifer, I can't wait to meet both of you. So, Merry Christmas to all of you, but Rhoda has to go because she might have bought herself a pecan pie, and it might be calling her name right now. So! This girl is out!"

27

IT WAS LATER THAT EVENING, not long before all of us were to meet in the living room for drinks before dinner was served, when Alex and I finished dressing.

"These cufflinks are killer," he said.

"And ironically, they've saved lives. Here, let me straighten your tie for you. Nice suit, by the way."

"You bought it for me."

"And it's a good fit—I like how it comes in close at the waist. And, God, here I go again. Just seeing you in a suit always makes me want to ditch everything and just get into bed with you. When it comes to you, I have such a suit fetish, it's not funny."

"I hear Santa wears a suit."

"Not the same thing."

"Turn around for me," he said. "Let me see what you're wearing."

I twirled around, and as I did, my ivory-colored Alexander McQueen gown with floral jewel embroidery fanned out. Tonight, I'd decided to wear my hair exactly as Alex loved it most—cascading down my back in a tumble of curls. And I was wearing the necklace and earrings he'd given to me earlier, which were spectacular.

"You like?"

"What's not to like—you look hot," he said. "How did I get so lucky?"

"When it comes to you, I ask myself that every day. Now, look," I said as I gave him a quick kiss on the lips. "I'm going to go see if Blackwell's suit fits her, as well as the shoes. And if they do, we'll be down to join the rest of you ASAP, OK?"

"You've got it."

~

"Hello?" I said when I knocked on Blackwell's bedroom door. "It's Jennifer. Are you dressed? May I come in?"

"Of course," Blackwell said. "The door's open. And please tell me that you've brought cases of champagne with you, because I believe that I might need a few glasses before tonight starts."

"How I wish that I did have some," I said as I stepped inside. And when she turned and we looked at each other, her lips parted at the same moment that I raised my hand to my own lips.

"Look at you!" Blackwell said. "Alex finally did it—he bought you the iconic Harry Winston diamond wreath necklace and the matching cascading diamond earrings. Oh, you lucky girl. So elegant! And your dress—perfection. As is your hair and makeup—Bernie has taught you well. You're going to be the star of the evening. Even I can't get over those jewels."

"I'm more than just lucky," I said. "I'm deeply in love."

"And yet none of your good fortune has changed you," she said. "You're still the feisty girl I met at our ruinous interview two years ago. None of it has gone to your head, and I can't tell you how much I admire you for that."

"I'm still a simple girl from the bowels of Maine," I said.

"Well, there's that..."

"And look at you," I said. "The suit fits! Do you like it?"

"I love it," she said. "It's striking. And the shoes are divoon. So, thank you, my dear. To think that you sketched out the suit and the shoes for me with a senior designer at Dior means more to me than you'll ever know, not to mention the sheer amount of time you spent to make this happen for me—and somehow without me even knowing about it. Now, come over here and give me a hug, because—and I will say this only to you—I might need one."

Blackwell needs a hug? What does that even mean?

"What's the matter?" I asked her as I crossed the room and gave her a hug. "Something's wrong. I sensed it at breakfast."

"Why don't we sit down on the bed? I think I need to have a good chat with someone whose opinion I hold in high esteem, and that would be yours."

"You can share anything with me," I said as I sat down beside her. "You know that I'm a vault."

"In fact, I do know that. You're one of the most trust-worthy and honorable people I know, especially when it comes to how you treat your friends. I'm fortunate to be among them."

"Why do you look so upset?"

"I think that I might be getting a little too old for this," she said. "I think I might have come to the point where I'm too cynical to enjoy any of it."

"What are you referring to?"

"Marcus," she said. "What he's seeking—or what he appears to be seeking. Is this just a weekend flirtation? Or is it something more substantial than that? I certainly don't know, and not knowing has rattled me. I don't know what to do with him. I'm conflicted, which I never am. You know me —always so confident. Always so certain. But I can tell you right now, that's not the person I am tonight."

I placed my hand over hers, and could feel the vulnerability coming off her in waves. I'd never seen her like this before. What on earth was she going through? "Talk to me," I said.

She did—and when she did, she opened up her heart to me.

"I've already had my chance at love, Jennifer," she said. "It was with Charles—he was my first and only, you know? And we were married for over twenty years. I thought that we'd be together forever, but look at how well that turned out—him cheating on me with the very woman he's married to now. And her name is Rita, for God's sake. Just imagine that—Charles going for a woman named Rita! And why did he do so? I know why. First, he obviously was tired of being with me. Second, she's a good ten years younger than I am, so what am I to make of that? That my shelf life is up at this point? Let's just be honest here—it might be up. I am, after all, in my mid-fifties. And how often does a woman in her mid-fifties find love?"

"All the time."

"Not for somebody with my standards, they don't. And don't ask me to lower them."

"I never would."

"What Charles did to me might have happened two years ago, but I'm here to tell you that it still stings. It still hurts. The deceit still lingers in ways that I should have shaken off a good year ago, but as much as I try to do so, I can't. At least not completely. I hate how he hurt not only me, but also our two daughters. I despise him for that. And yet somehow, throughout our marriage and right up to the very end when all of his lies were revealed, I trusted him with all of my heart. So tell me this—how am I to trust anyone again after what that sonofabitch did to me? I'm not sure that I can. And yet Marcus is bound and determined to come here again tonight to see me. I've tried my best not to lead him on, but that's been nothing short of an unmitigated failure, because I admit it—I do find him attractive. He's bright, he's funny, he's good looking, and he's interesting." She sighed. "I'm at a loss."

"What you need to become is the person you were before Charles," I said.

"I don't even know who that woman was at this point. We all change with age—I certainly have. All of us are altered by our experiences, our triumphs, and our challenges, and by the accumulation of our disappointments. Charles gutted me. What if another man does the same thing to me, whether it's Marcus or somebody else? How am I going to get through that? What I'm facing tonight really has nothing to do with Marcus—he's a lovely man. And I sense that he could be a good man. But what if I'm wrong and he isn't? What if it's all smoke and mirrors when it comes to him? What I'm facing tonight has to do with trusting someone again. Allowing someone in beyond the fortress I've built around myself over these past two years. You and Alex and my daughters are perhaps the only people in my life who know who I really am as a person. Many rightfully see me as a full-on bitch known and feared as the façade that is 'Blackwell'. And I take full responsibility for that. But those closest to me know that there's another side to me, and it's that side that was blindsided the moment I met Marcus. It's not fair for me to play along with him if I'm feeling like this. So, when he arrives tonight, I've decided to just shut down whatever has been brewing between us once and for all. For his sake—and also for my own."

"Are you sure? Barbara, it's so clear to all of us that you two have a connection. And you must know that something like that just doesn't come around very often. Are you sure that you want to throw that away just because you're scared that he might hurt you?"

"I see no need to go through being hurt again."

"Who's to say he will hurt you? And how do you even know if anything *will* come of this? You've only known each other for three days—how much weight can either of you put on that? Both of you are in the midst of a try-out phase, so just listen to me. You yourself have said that he's a bright, funny, good-looking, and interesting man. Isn't that worth exploring? Don't you deserve to at least see where this goes? It might go nowhere—and fine, if it doesn't, both of you will know sooner rather than later, and you'll just move on with no hard feelings. You'll just part ways. But what if there *is* something between you two? How can you possibly deny yourself of that? You're still a young woman."

"The hell I am."

"Fine, you might not be Daniella's age, but does that mean there isn't a partner out there for you who is your age? Does one's love life end at mid-life? I think we both know better. I believe that Marcus has said that he'd been cheated on by his own wife. What kind of scars do you think that left on him? And yet look at him now—making an effort to get back into the game with a woman he finds attractive, funny —and from the looks of what I've seen on his face today and last night—stylish, and beautiful. Yes, he's only known you for a few days, but I can tell you this—the moment I met Alex in that elevator after my disastrous interview with you, it was like lightning struck me. I don't know how or where it came from, but there was an instant attraction and connection. And then there was the way that he helped me pick up my flyaway resumes. How gallant was that? The rest is history when it comes to Alex and me, but still, consider how we came to be. I didn't make any of it easy for him at first because I'm nothing if not bull-headed, but eventually I let down my guard—and look at how well that turned out. We're not only married, but we're crazy in love with each other. So, why can't the same happen for you? Why would you ever deny yourself a second chance—especially one that might turn out to be better than what you experienced with Charles?"

"As I said, I'm scared," she said in a low voice. "Because I think that my time for finding love again has passed."

And when she said that, I knew that Blackwell had once again just bared her soul to me. She really did believe that her time was up when it came to meeting someone who might eventually come to love her. She was in a dark place right now.

And it was my job to lift her out of it.

"What do you have to lose from getting to know Marcus?" I asked.

"Just getting to know him? Nothing, I suppose."

"Then how about if you just start there? Do you think that he's worth the trouble? If not, then I do agree with you —move on. But right now, if we just forget about what Charles did to you and focus on your initial impressions of Marcus, what do you feel inside? When you strip Charles away, do you really believe that you should be finished with Marcus? Or do you think that when all of us are back in Manhattan, that you should see him a few more times, and decide where you go from there? Look, I get that you have every reason to be scared and to feel vulnerable after what you've been through, but don't let your fear of starting over again derail what might be the best thing that has ever happened to you. Because this might be it, Barbara. You're attracted to him, which is great. What's better is that your attraction isn't just physical, but also intellectual. Being open to possibilities doesn't equate a commitment, wouldn't you agree?"

"I suppose it doesn't."

"How long has Marcus been divorced from his wife?"

"Five years."

"Then all the better, because none of this can be considered a rebound situation for either of you. That period is long gone. So, how about just proceeding with caution, but also with a fair bit of willingness to be open to him and to give him a chance? Because while you might not believe it, Barbara, you do deserve a second chance. You deserve to have a partner in your life, to have someone to go home to and to grow old with. If Marcus turns out not to be the one, then fine—onward you go. But if he is the one, think about the implications. You will be able to enjoy an entirely new life. My suggestion is that you let go of Charles and every rotten thing he ever did to you, and move forward. The past is the past, and you're facing a potentially exciting new present. It's time for you to tend to yourself and your own happiness. Screw Charles, because Marcus might be the one who leads you to a happier future."

"He is rather something," she said as she squeezed my hand.

"Then see what comes of it," I said. "If it's nothing, move on. And even if it does come to that, then your takeaway is this—you've still triumphed because at least you can say to yourself that you did give it an effort and that you are open to more opportunities when and if they should come."

"As if they'll come," she said.

I kissed her on the cheek. "They will if you allow them to. But why not start with Marcus first? It's only been three days—what harm can come from getting to know him better? It's not as if you're completely invested in him at this point. You've both just started this journey of yours."

"I will say this," she said. "He's going to have to pursue me—it sure as hell isn't going to be the other way around. I come from a completely different generation than you do, Jennifer. I will not chase after him. If he wants to spend time with me, then he's going to have to work for it. And when I say that, I don't mean that he's going to have to work hard. I just mean that he's going to have to engage me as the gentleman he's already revealed himself to be. I'm old-fashioned when it comes to those sorts of things. If he wants to be with me, then he's going to have to show me that he wants to be with me."

"Fair enough. And since he's around your age, I'd actually expect that from him."

"I'll demand it."

"But hasn't he already done so?" I asked. "I mean, come on—you haven't been pursuing him at all since we've been here. Instead, he's been pursuing you."

She looked thoughtful for a moment when I said that, and then she just shrugged. "I guess he has been."

"Men," I said as I leaned back on the bed. "And relationships. Why do so many of us have to deal with the kind of insecurities that surround both, no matter how strong we think we are as women?"

"Good question."

"Well, here's your answer—it's because we're human.

And you're human, Barbara. Follow your heart tonight. Be spontaneous. Take risks. Become alive again. If he surprises you, surprise him right back. Breakfast was a bit stiff between you two this morning, but you can fix that now. All of what happens next is up to you, because I can tell you that he's already there, ready and waiting. So, what do you want? Have a think about that before we go downstairs. In the meantime, I'm going to haul my fat ass off this bed and give you a hug and a kiss, and tell you that I love you. So, come on—that's right. Get up off the bed and give me a hug and a couple of air kisses. I might call you my surrogate womb in jest, but you truly are the mother I never had. And I do love you, Barbara. I only want the best for you."

"You were wonderful just now, you know?"

"I only spoke from my heart."

At that point, the time occurred to me, and I looked down at my watch. "It's late," I said. "Marcus might already be here at this point. Are you ready to do this?"

"First, I need to check myself in a mirror, because my eyes might have become a bit bright during certain parts of our conversation."

"Take your time."

When she emerged from the bathroom a few minutes later, I saw the Blackwell that I knew and loved—strong and confident, and with a sparkle of mischief in her eyes.

"All right," she said. "Let's do this, because you're right. I became nearly paralyzed because I was overthinking all of this. So, thank you for talking me off the cliff, my dear girl. You're wise beyond your years, which is one of the things that I've always admired about you. So, game on. Let's see what comes of this."

"Give me your hand," I said.

"Why? So you can give me the flu? An STD? Rickets?"

Oh, she's so back now...

"Just give it to me."

She gave it to me.

"We're going to enter that room together," I said. "And don't think for one single moment that I won't ever have your back."

~

IT WAS ten minutes past seven when we entered the living room, and while there was no sign of Marcus, Justin was just coming through the front door and moving into the vestibule. Because the snow was still falling heavily outside, his black overcoat was covered in snow, which Alex brushed off him as Alexa stepped forward to greet him.

"You made it," she said.

"I know that you're leaving tomorrow, and no amount of snow was about to keep me from seeing you again." He stopped for a moment and looked at her in her red evening dress. "You look beautiful, Alexa. That's some dress."

"Thank you," she said. "And you look very handsome, Justin."

Alex helped him out of his coat.

"Thank you, Mr. Wenn," he said.

"Remember, it's Alex."

When Justin shrugged off his coat, Alex swept it away—and then it was just he and Alexa standing in the vestibule.

"How was your day on the slopes?" she asked.

"Do you really want to know?"

"Sure..."

"As embarrassing as this is going to sound, I was consumed by thoughts of you, I was more than a bit distracted. Generally, I'm an excellent skier, but today, I fell so often, my buddies thought I was drunk."

"I'm in love with him already," I heard Daniella—who was standing to my right—say softly. Cutter was standing next to her in a black suit with a cobalt-blue tie that matched the color of his eyes—and his hand was pressed against the small of her back, which suggested to me that whatever was happening between those two was only moving forward.

"You look cold," Alexa said to Justin. "Come inside. We have a fire roaring in the living room. It's warmer in here."

"Not just yet," he said. "Because I'm not sure if you know this, but hanging right above you is mistletoe. So, you know, that's not only a tradition I need to follow through with, but let's just say that it's another way for me to warm up."

When he said that, he leaned forward and gave Alexa a chaste kiss on the lips that was so sensitive and delicate, my heart reached out for each of them—especially for Alexa. She needed something like this, especially after having all of Daniella's repeated conquests rammed down her throat for years.

"Sorry," he said when they parted.

"Don't be," she said.

"I hope I wasn't too forward," he said. "I couldn't help myself." He looked around at all of us. "I promise that I meant no disrespect. I just think that Alexa is extraordinary. And since today might be my last day with her, I wanted to seal it with a kiss. I owe that to whomever hung the mistletoe."

"Well, you *are* studying medicine at NYU," Blackwell said. "And since Alexa is fresh out of college and is now living in the city with me, certainly you two can see one another again. Soon, Alexa plans to find an apartment of her own because she's interested in working at Wenn Environmental. And from what I hear, Wenn Environmental is interested in working with her. So, I have a feeling that this won't be the last time that you see my daughter. And I have to say that I approve of the gesture, Justin, because doing that took guts, especially since you were doing so in front of her mother. And by the way, just look at you—dressed in a Burberry suit for the evening. And so clean-cut. I'm very happy that you're here."

"Thank you, Mrs. Blackwell."

"It's Barbara."

"Well, then thank you, Barbara."

"Now kiss my daughter again," Blackwell said. "Because schedules are difficult—and neither of you know when you'll even see each other again."

"Seriously?" Justin said.

"Go for it," Alexa said.

"Yes, go for it," Daniella encouraged.

And man, did that boy ever go for it. With one fell swoop, Alexa was properly dipped and kissed. When they finally came up for air and righted themselves, Alexa looked as if she was about to faint.

"Somebody needs to get these two a drink," Alex said. "STAT!"

~

"WHY ISN'T HE HERE YET?" Barbara said to me as one of the servers brought each of us another martini. Christmas dinner was ready to go, and the catering staff had returned to serve it to us—along with pre-dinner drinks. "He's twenty minutes late, for God's sake. What could be the hold up?"

"I'm sure that there's a very good reason," I said.

"It could have been breakfast," she said. "I wasn't exactly at my best."

"Or it could be the snow. Have you seen how it's piling up outside? Relax—he'll be here. And don't forget that he manages a hedge fund, for God's sake. There are ridiculous pressures when it comes to tending to something like that. Who knows what might have come up for him today?"

"Well, at the very least, he could have had the decency to call."

"But I'm not sure that he has any of our numbers. Does he have yours? Because I know that he doesn't have mine."

"Do you really think that I'd give out my number so easily?"

"Then there's your answer. Something must have happened, and because none of us thought of exchanging numbers, he's clearly unable to reach us. Marcus has been nothing if not a gentleman since we met him. I'm fairly certain that he would have called if he'd had any of our numbers. So, let's just settle down, mix and enjoy our martinis, and wait for him to come. Because he will come. You'll see."

"My stomach is in knots," she said. "I'm terrified. A part of me doesn't want him to come."

"Remember our conversation," I said.

She took a deep breath and nodded at me. "You're right. It's time to move on. It's time to let someone else in, even if that makes me want to throw up, which you can't repeat to anyone—ever."

"You know that I won't. Whatever you've told me about how you're feeling right now is strictly between us."

"I'm a wreck."

"But a beautiful one. Now, take a sip of your martini—liquid courage and all that."

She did, and then she checked her watch. "We can't hold up dinner forever. All of you worked so hard on what you've provided for us tonight. And heaven knows that nobody wants a dry bird, so we can't let that happen."

"The bird in question is swaddled in tinfoil," I said. "That alone will help it to reabsorb its juices. I've got this. I promise you that it won't be dry."

"Now you sound like that fat Contessa woman."

"Yes, and I believe that she's the one who saved your ass last year?"

"OK, so fine, she did."

I nodded at her drink. "We'll give him fifteen more minutes. If he doesn't show, then we'll have dinner. So, in the meantime, just take another long, cool sip from your cocktail and enjoy it. Consider it medicine."

"It is rather therapeutic," she said.

"You think?" I saw the tension on her face, so I put my arm around her waist and leaned into her. "He'll be here," I said close to her ear. "He's not about to stand my mother up. So, we can either run this into the ground if you want, or we can distract ourselves by going over to say hello to Madison and Brock. We haven't even spoken to them yet, which is beyond rude."

"Fine."

"Hi, good-lookings," I said as we approached them.

"Jennifer, your necklace and your earrings are amazing," Madison said. "Holy God! I've been admiring them since you and Barbara first entered the room. They're as beautiful as your dress."

"Which actually fits her ass," Blackwell said. "So, let's all have a moment of silence for that."

"Thank you, Madison," I said, overlooking Blackwell's comment—even though I was happy to hear her being herself again because it meant that she was coming back into herself. "The necklace and the earrings were my over-the-top Christmas gift from Alex. I love them."

"They're kind of mesmerizing," Brock said. "I don't know much about diamonds, but those look as if they've been set on fire. My cousin sure knows how to bring it."

"That he does," I said. "But enough about that. Have you two had fun today?"

"We've had a terrific day. From the presents to breakfast and to cooking dinner for everyone with Alex and you, it's been a blast. And now all of us have gathered to eat dinner together. I personally want to thank you and Alex for that, Jennifer," Brock said. "You've made my first Christmas with Madison something that I'll remember for the rest of my life."

"Well," Blackwell said. "Even I have to admit that that was beyond romantic. Because what I heard in your voice is that you clearly did mean that, Brock. So, may you two carry on. You're a lovely couple."

"Your suit is amazing, Barbara," Madison said. "Just look at how well it fits. And the detailing is sublime. It's so you."

"And so it is," she said. "Jennifer outdid herself. And because she did, I have to say that I don't even miss Chanel right now. I'm delighted to be wearing something new—and something that was made especially for me. Talk about couture," she said. "I've never been blessed with something quite like this."

"You're a knockout," I said.

"I hope that I am," she said, and in her voice, I heard the underlying meaning in what she said. She wanted to make an impression on Marcus when he came—if he did come. Where was he? He was nearly thirty minutes late at this point. Soon, I'd have to just throw in the towel and get to

Christmas dinner, because I needed to respect all of the work that Alex, Madison, Brock, and I had done today.

I was in a total quandary about when to pull the trigger and was about to conclude that Marcus might not come after all when Daniella said, "Hey! Here comes Marcus!"

Praise Jesus...

She and Cutter were standing next to the wall of windows that overlooked the house's entrance. She lifted up a hand to wave at him through the windows, and when she did, I took Blackwell's hand, excused us from Brock and Madison, and quickly spoke to her.

"Do whatever feels natural," I said. "He's late for a reason. He'll tell us what that reason is when he steps inside. He's no fool—he knows very well that he's late—and he'll likely be filled with apologies because of it. So, let him apologize, and if his excuse sounds valid, then immediately let him off the hook for all of it. OK?"

"I'm terrified right now."

"Why?"

"Because we leave tomorrow. I might not see him again. And I think that I might want to see him again. But what if he doesn't feel that same? What if this is it? This is why I've never put my heart on the line again, Jennifer. At my age, going through this sort of bullshit is hell."

"He lives in Manhattan. I believe that you also live there. If you want to see him again, then make him want to see you again."

"And how on earth am I to do that?"

"Just be yourself. Follow through with whatever your gut tells you."

"And I've already told you that my gut wants to throw up."

"Well, I'd highly recommend that you keep that shit at

bay," I said. "Otherwise, you'll need a mint, which unfortunately I don't have on me."

"He has flowers," Daniella said. "And the snow is so heavy, it's pelting him, the poor guy."

Alex went to the door and opened it. And when he did, Blackwell's grip on my hand turned into a talon.

"Relax," I said.

"Impossible."

"He's here for you, not for the rest of us. Think about that for a moment. So what if he's late? Something important must have held him up, and there could be very good reasons for that, which I believe we'll hear because, as you've noted, he is a gentleman and will want to let all of us know why he's late. What matters is that he showed up. So, you know, let's go over and greet him without any attitude."

"Attitude?" she said. "I have no attitude. In fact, I think I'm about to faint."

"Why?"

"Because I'm about to take your advice and let myself go. That's terrifying to me."

"Then turn your terror into electricity," I said. "Get your spine back. Just be yourself, because that's clearly the woman he's attracted to. You've been your unreasonable self ever since you met him, and look at how he's responded to that. He gets a kick out of it. He's told you that you make him laugh. He's clearly enchanted by you. Now, go over there and greet him."

"Oh, holy hell!"

"Hello, Marcus," Alex said as Marcus walked through the front door and entered the vestibule. "I'm happy that you're here."

"I apologize that I'm late," he said as he shook Alex's hand. "I would have called, but I didn't have anyone's number. And that's my mistake—it's on me because I should have asked for Barbara's number this morning at breakfast, but for whatever reason, it didn't occur to me. So, I'm sorry for any inconvenience that I might have caused all of you. I know that I've held up dinner, and I'm very sorry for that."

"There's been no inconvenience," I said.

"I think that you're just being kind, Jennifer, but thank you for that," he said.

"Those are some flowers you're holding," I said.

"At breakfast, I asked you what Barbara's favorite flowers were. You told me that they were white peonies. So I started to call around to see if I could find them, first to the local florist, which was a bust. But since I'm nothing if not determined, I got on the Internet and found a shop in Portland that had them in stock, if you can believe that. It took me a good hour or so to find them, and when I did, I had to convince the owner to open the shop and then I had find a driver who was willing to bring them to me in this weather. That's why I'm so late. I regret that. But these flowers were important to me, and since I knew they were on the way, I had to wait for them. They were just delivered to me about ten minutes ago. And now I'm here with them." He looked over at Blackwell. "So I could give them to you," he said.

I pressed my hand against her back and gently moved her toward him.

"They're lovely," she said. "And they are indeed my favorite. Just look at them—it's like spring again. How did you ever find peonies in December?"

"What matters is that I did."

"Let me brush the snow off your coat," Alex said. "You're covered in it."

When Alex was finished, he took Marcus' coat and placed it in the nearby coat closet.

"Thank you," Marcus said to Alex. "And it's good to see all of you again. I want to thank all of you for turning what I thought was going to be a lonely holiday into a holiday to remember. I can't tell you how appreciative I am that you've opened your home to me. And to see Barbara again—two times in one day. It's like a gift. You leave tomorrow, right?"

"We do," she said.

"Then tonight's the night," he said.

"What does that even mean?"

"Look above you," he said. "I noticed it the moment I stepped inside. Mistletoe."

"Oh, that," she said. "Well, just so you know, it's already been used by my daughter and her new suitor before you arrived, so its magical powers are moot at this point."

He cocked his head at her. "Are they?"

And with that, Marcus Koch took Blackwell's hands in his own and pulled her toward him so that he could seal the deal with a kiss full on her lips. And when he did that, the room gasped, because nobody was expecting him to go there so quickly—or for her to allow him to.

But she did—and I was so proud of her that I started to tear up. She could have pulled away if she'd wanted to, but she didn't. Instead, she threw caution to the wind—just as I'd suggested—and gave herself over to him in ways that looked searing. When those two kissed—they kissed.

"Well," she said when their lips parted. "I don't know what to say, other than that my lipstick is all over your lips and that you might look as if you're in drag. So, here, let me clean that up for you, because you can't go on looking like that tonight. At this point, you'll get lipstick on the turkey."

"Yes I can," he said. "Because maybe I like your lips on mine."

And when he said that, he went in for the kill again, but

this time his kiss was deeper and more passionate than the one that had preceded it.

With his arm wrapped around Blackwell's waist, he pulled her in so close to him that he was able to plant the kind of kiss on her that shook the room into silence. When he released himself from her, I watched as they searched each other's eyes, and then I looked at Daniella and Alexa to see their reactions, which I knew would be important to Blackwell.

And I was relieved when I did so.

Daniella's head was resting against Cutter's chest, her eyes were bright with tears, her lips were trembling—and Cutter was there for her. His right arm was strong around her waist and he was holding her steady as she tried to take all of this in.

As for Alexa, she was standing in front of Justin, who knew nothing about the magnitude that was unfolding between Blackwell and Marcus right now, but he nevertheless was sensitive enough to support Alexa with a hand on her shoulder when she welled up and suddenly put her face in her hands.

"Oh, my God," Daniella said.

"Right?" Alexa said, her own eyes wet with tears.

"Is this even happening?"

"I think it is. Mom so deserves this."

"Totes to the real!"

"Well," Blackwell said as she pulled away from Marcus and lifted his hair away from his forehead. "Apparently, we've just caused something of a stink."

"It would seem that way," he said. "And under the fragrant mistletoe, no less. Who saw that coming?"

She placed the palm of her hand against the side of his

cheek, looked into his eyes, and said, "Let's just say that I'm happy that it did."

She turned to look at all of us. And when she did, I could see by the light in her eyes that she'd succeeded in shedding all of her fear, and that she was now willing to give herself the second chance she hadn't thought she deserved. Would something substantial come from this? Who knew?

What mattered most was that Blackwell had made a conscious decision to toss aside her fears about being a divorced woman in her mid-fifties who, in her mind, might not be worthy of finding love again. To me, that sounded ridiculous, but to her, it was so real, it had nearly been paralyzing.

And yet she'd done it.

She'd listened to me, she'd taken my advice, she'd buckled down, and she'd kissed Marcus not just once, but twice—and in front of all of us, no less. That alone told me that she was ready to move forward with her life, and perhaps to find the right man to spend the rest of her life with.

Hopefully, Marcus would be that man. But if he wasn't, I knew from Blackwell's actions alone that she was at last free from Charles and his deceit, and that she was ready to move forward when the right man came along.

If he hadn't already.

AFTERWORD

Can't wait for my next steamy book? More are coming, and finding out when is an easy fix! Join me on Facebook by searching for Christina Ross Author and especially join my SPAM-free email blast on my website: christinaross.net. By simply joining my email blast, you'll never miss another book—or the opportunity to receive an ARC to review a book before it goes live to the public.

I love to hear from my readers! Would you like more of the *Annihilate Me* series? The *Ignite Me* series? Or the *Unleash Me* series? Please let me know at: christinarossauthor@gmail.com. I hope to hear from you soon!

If you would leave a review of this or any of my books, I'd appreciate it. Reviews are critical to every writer. Please leave even the shortest of reviews. And thank you for doing so!

XO,
    Christina